So Pucking Over It

Rush Hockey #3

Elise Faber

SO PUCKING OVER IT
BY ELISE FABER
Newsletter sign-up

Rush Hockey

ONE

AXEL

S moke and ash.

Heat radiating up off the asphalt.

Abandoned cars stuck, literally *stuck* to the road, tires melted, metal rims coated with ash and oxides, windows shattered, exteriors reduced to rusted steel frames.

Car after car after *car*.

But no trucks. No trailers.

No sign of the woman I loved.

Embers still coated the air, choking me worse than the panic that had gripped me from the moment I'd seen the news reports, that continued to claw and twist and shred my insides as more and more time went on without hearing from her.

Hot air singeing my throat, burning my skin.

Had she felt this?

Had she felt a hundred times worse as the flames had closed in?

Heat licking ever nearer, the roar of the fire and wind giving way to this quiet, this eerie, mournful silence.

This...*death*.

I stared out at the hills, once covered with long, slender stalks of grass that whispered in the breeze. Those hills were now black and smoking, something out of a shitty Hollywood dystopian movie.

Except, this was real life.

Except, the woman I loved had been right in the middle of this.

Except...the woman I loved hadn't been heard or seen from since.

And my heart, the one that had shed all the chains and armor keeping itself safe, the vulnerable organ that had opened and accepted my woman, had loved her with everything I was, had hoped, had pleaded with the fates, with the universe that this would be the first time in my fucking life that I actually got to keep the good in it.

Instead, the universe had sent us a big *fuck you.*

It had sent flames closing in on this town.

Fire tornados spinning through the superheated air.

Houses reduced to nothing but chimneys and concrete foundations.

Street signs melted.

Parks and trees turned to ash.

And my woman...was gone.

Gone.

All while the rest of the world continued to spin onward.

Two

AXEL

Hockey was life.

Hockey was everything I had, all I'd *ever* had.

It was something I'd loved and hated, almost in equal measure over the years—hating the grind, the travel, the way the long seasons could close in on me, hating the commitment it took, the gym time, the off-ice training, the volunteer work and meetings and watching tape, hating that it wasn't easy, that the hours weren't regular.

But the love always came back around to smother the hate.

Love of the cool rink air prickling over my skin, sinking down through my jersey, finding the gaps in my pads. Love for the cheers of the crowd, the high when I connected a really good pass with a teammate, when I scored or crushed one of the motherfuckers on the other team into the boards and most especially when that fucker deserved it.

Though, I was equal opportunity.

Take the hits, dish them out, so long as I didn't mar this pretty face.

Bailey liked it.

Bailey—

I closed my eyes, dropping onto the side of the bed in the cheap ass motel. It was the only place I'd been able to get a room, the only place within fifty miles of River's Bend, California that had space for me.

The rest were under evacuation as the firefighters continued to get the fire under control or were filled with evacuees.

I knew because I'd gone to every single one in search of Bailey.

I knew because I'd gone to every single shelter between here and River's Bend.

Phones weren't working this close to the fire, and I hadn't seen one glimpse of Bailey's big truck, of Bailey's curvy body that I'd worshipped every inch of. I hadn't heard her voice or her laugh or watched her smile that special smile she saved just for me, her brown eyes warming to liquid chocolate.

But I'd found a place to stay.

I'd get a few hours of sleep, would get back on the road, searching.

Not stopping until I found her.

Not stopping until the hope inside me was incinerated, reduced to ashes like the trees and houses out there.

Not stopping until there was nothing left inside me.

Because my heart hadn't actually beat until I'd met Bailey. I hadn't truly lived, not until I'd been lucky enough to love her.

So, hockey didn't matter.

I didn't give a fuck that final game in the series was two days away from now.

It was a dream that existed in another life altogether.

Because Bailey was my dream now.

And I just had to hold tight to the tiny bundle of hope still flickering with life in my heart, had to carefully shield it, to keep it alive.

Because without it, the man I was—Axel Finnegan, professional hockey player, reformed fuck-up with a heart that couldn't be cracked open...

Well, he would cease to exist.

And I was terrified to see what sort of monster I would turn into.

My eyes were gritty when I woke to my alarm two hours later.

The smell of smoke clung to the air, to my clothes, my skin, my hair.

But I was awake and dawn was approaching, and I needed to get moving. I pulled out the printout of the map—Brit's idea before she'd driven me to the airport directly from the game, not blinking an eye when I'd said I needed to leave immediately.

None of them had.

Pierre, the owner of the Gold and Rush hockey teams, had offered his private plane, had it fueled and ready to take off by the time I made it to the airport.

And Brit had promised to hold down the fort, no matter if I made it back for the game, and on that front not *one* member of the coaching staff, of the support staff, not *one* teammate had made a comment, other than to offer their help.

Because they knew that family was the most important thing.

And Bailey was mine.

So I looked at the map, at the printout that Dani had run into the locker room and stowed in my bag as I'd gotten dressed—brought thanks to that idea of Brit's—and picked the next section I was going to start with.

I'd covered the western route into River's Bend in the few hours remaining of the day before, thinking it had been the easiest path out of town, considering where the ranch was located.

But I hadn't been able to get through to the ranch, not with all the abandoned cars, the smoke and ash and utter destruction.

River's Bend was destroyed.

I'd seen that much.

The beautiful downtown with the historic buildings that were supposed to be the backdrop to the Summer Festival in just two weeks' time were gone. Monroe's, where I'd finally made my move, finally given in to the draw between Bailey and myself was also gone. As was the park where I'd snuck kisses. The apartment building that I'd sublet.

Gone.

All of it.

Gone.

I worried about Bailey. I worried about her horse, Data, her cow, Picard, her dog, Spock, knowing she wouldn't leave the pets she loved behind. I worried about her cattle, the herd that was her livelihood, and the poor animals were probably scattered and scared and maybe dead. I worried about Billie Rose and Dessie, the women I had to thank for my heart belonging to Bailey. I worried about my former teammates, whose season was over, but those that had property in town would have been in River's Bend when the fire broke out.

I worried. *Period.*

It sat heavy on my soul, was a knot of barbed wire in my gut, making it difficult for me to think, to focus.

Especially, as more time went on without a word from Bailey, without contact.

All while the fire burned on.

But...I couldn't focus on that.

It would paralyze me. It would make it impossible for me to focus on finding the woman I loved.

So, I shoved the worry down, smothered it until it was buried deeply in the back of my mind.

I could allow the nightmares to come later.

Mind settled, I folded the map, set it next to my cell. Then I took a quick shower to get the ash off, to rid myself of the smoky scent that was seemingly embedded into my cells.

Ten minutes later, I was grabbing my shit and going back out to my car.

And I was driving toward the rising sun, the midnight navy of the early morning sky glowing with a narrow swathe of orange above the hills in the distance.

I searched.

I scoured every inch south of River's Bend for any sign of a big, old truck, of shining brown hair and the woman I loved.

But I still didn't find Bailey.

THREE

BAILEY

I didn't know where I was.

Didn't know what time it was, not with the smoke so heavy in the air, so heavy that I could barely breathe.

Everything burned—my exposed skin had been scalded and blistered from the flames, my lungs were on fire with every breath. I'd tied a spare sweatshirt around my face, trying to prevent further inhalation, but it hadn't—*didn't*—do much. Not with the smoke still choking me, stinging my eyes, the unnatural heat in the air suffocating me.

There were so many unknowns—was I moving the wrong way or the right one? Toward the fire or away? Would I find water soon? I *had* to find water soon.

I'd been searching for a stream, for any water source for a while now as I made my way down the narrow trail that had been my savior, but I hadn't yet had any luck. Partly, because it was hard to see. Hell, I couldn't tell if it was day or night or somewhere in between.

So, it was impossible to know if the orange glow was from the sun shining through the smoke, or if it was even more flames in the distance.

And it was silent.

A deadly sort of quiet that was absent of the sound of insects, of birds and critters. No cars. No other people.

Just me in the smoke-filled hills.

The only peace I could find in my current surroundings was the fact that it *was* quiet.

The roaring of the flames, louder than I could have ever imagined, weren't bearing down on me any longer.

Not like they had when I'd been trapped on the road south of town, blocked off from the other routes, trying to get out through any possible means.

Somehow, I'd managed to get us all to safety—me, Picard, Data, and Spock—but it had nearly killed me. Literally. I'd barely managed to get Picard and Data harnessed and out of the trailer, the wildness of the flames spooking them, making them not want to leave the false safety of their rolling enclosure. I'd barely been able to get them out of the trailer and then to stop them from running into the chaos of the road, the flames, before the wildfire had closed in near enough to blister the skin of my hands and bared arms, to singe my hair.

Not to mention, leading a horse, a cow, and a dog (and myself) through a smoke-filled, flame-lined road and into the surrounding hills and doing it while we were all freaked the *fuck* out (including myself) had been a goddamned miracle.

I didn't want to risk riding Data, not when we didn't have water and it was taking so much effort to keep them calm.

I might get thrown and that could be a death sentence, especially if I was injured.

And I might need Data's strength later.

For now, though, we were okay. I was moving downhill, hoping that was taking me away from the fire, hoping the flames would keep moving in a direction that wasn't toward me.

I couldn't outrun it.

I had to get away from it.

I had to—

The wind picked up, rustling through the trees surrounding us. Their branches and trunks were untouched, at least for the moment. But the rush of air drifting through the ends of my hair, over my skin was hot and other worldly and—

Spock whined.

"It's okay," I said, keeping my voice soft, even though I was the only one here, even though there wasn't another soul nearby to tell me to be quiet.

I scratched his head, thankful that he was a good listener, that he'd stayed right at my side through this insanity—though, if I could tell him to go, to get to safety, I would in a heartbeat.

He whined again, and I straightened. "I know," I whispered. "We need to keep moving."

So I kept walking, kept picking my way down the trail, kept helping Data and Picard navigate the rocky and oftentimes steep path, kept Spock close.

Calm voice.

Calm body.

Calm movements.

But none of us were buying it.

The air was too stagnant, too still. The smoke wasn't lessening. It was...growing thicker, heavier, pushing on us.

Or maybe, it was that my lungs weren't working as well?

Maybe the heaviness growing in my feet wasn't because fatigue had reached up to grab me tightly, to tug at my ankles and legs, to make my footsteps grow unsteady.

Maybe it was because my body was shutting down, with my mind not far behind it.

How many hours had I been walking?

How long had I been running?

A *long* time, I thought.

Or it could be that there wasn't enough oxygen in the air, that I *couldn't breathe. I couldn't breathe.* I was being smothered. I—

Spock whined again and I jerked, managed to snap myself out of my panic.

"Calm, Bay," I murmured, giving myself the same gentle tone my pets were getting, forcing myself to focus on the words, even though they were a lie when I added, "You've been in worse scrapes than this. You'll be fine." A breath that sent me coughing so hard that I bent in half, the force of the wheezing taking my hands to my knees. "You'll be fine," I rasped out again when I'd managed to stop hacking.

I paused to tie the sweatshirt I'd secured around my face a little tighter, folding it again, trying for another layer between my nose and mouth and the smoke.

"Fine," I whispered again.

Except, even as that word crossed my lips, I hit a loose patch of rocks and my feet slid out from under me.

I managed—just barely—to have the forethought to release the ropes on Data and Picard's halters, so as not to take them down with me.

But that was all I could do as I collided hard with the ground, began to slide down the steep hill.

Spock barked, and Data whinnied in surprise.

But I couldn't get any words out, not when my already damaged lungs couldn't draw in enough air, not when rocks and dirt were scraping my back, shredding the skin of my bare arms.

Eventually, I slid to a stop, pain intruding on every single one of my nerves.

"Fuck," I whispered, just lying there for a minute, trying to get my breath back, trying to summon the energy to get up.

Rocks skittering.

Spock appearing at my side, gently licking my face.

"Hi, buddy." I managed to lift my arm, to scratch his ears. "I'm okay."

Nothing about this was okay, least of all my bruised and battered body.

But I had to keep telling myself that, had to keep moving.

Blood trickled down my nose, and I realized I'd lost my makeshift mask somewhere along the fall. I couldn't see it as I looked up at the hill I'd slipped down, so there was nothing to be done about it. The path was steep, and I didn't have time to waste looking for a sweatshirt that was hardly helping. I just had to hope I could get Picard and Data down it.

Swallowing hard, I began inching my way up, beyond thankful when Data started taking careful steps toward me.

"Come on, baby," I coaxed, helping her over a particularly slippery portion of the trail.

Finally, though, we both made it to the bottom.

"Good girl," I murmured, rubbing the spot between her eyes. "Wait here, okay?"

She huffed and I turned back to the hill, summoned the energy to make my way back up to Picard who was stomping nervously at the top.

"Come on, honey," I said, grabbing his rope halter and trying to draw him forward.

He dug in his hoofs.

"We gotta go, baby." More stern now.

A soft, protesting *moo*.

Grunting, I tugged harder. "*Come. On.*" Another tug, but then I heard something that I made ice cold daggers dig into my spine.

I froze, horror collecting in my belly as the telltale rumble grew.

What I heard was death.

And it was coming for me.

Again.

Four

Axel

The hours were passing me by—too fucking fast.

Each mile closer back to River's Bend brought landscape that looked increasingly more and more like it belonged in a post-apocalyptic novel.

Blackened tree trunks, barren branches, smoking ground.

Brown and orange-hued air.

Twisted rebar and bare foundations were all that remained of every house I could see.

The hotel the visiting teams would stay in when they drove up to play the Rush had been reduced to a pile of blackened beams, floors having collapsed and gone topsy-turvy, leaving it to look like a fucked-up house of cards.

I drove over the bridge that led toward River's Bend, ignoring the lights from the sheriff's cruisers that were blocking the route into town up ahead.

I was getting in.

I was getting to the ranch.

Because Bailey hadn't been at any of the hospitals, not at any of the police stations or fire departments or churches or school gymnasiums. She wasn't in any of the shelters.

So she was here.

And I was going to find her.

The bridge thrummed with its familiar vibration as I drove over the steel and concrete. The river was extremely low after a dry winter and spring, mostly exposed gravel and riverbed at this point in the year. That dry weather was most certainly why everything had gone up like so much tinder.

The banks that were normally covered with thick green oaks— save for a narrow trail on River's Bend's side of the waterway that people used to access the water—were now unrecognizable. Normally, during the summer and on weekends, there were kids splashing and skipping rocks and generally just making a ruckus, their adults supervising, or for the few early souls who were up with the sun (which didn't include me—anytime I'd seen fisherman it had been when I was heading to bed, not getting out of it), standing in the waist-deep water fishing for rainbow trout.

But all of that was gone now.

An empty river due to the drought.

The trees surrounding it all but sticks of tinder. The ground blackened and devoid of vegetation. The trail and its wooden handrail reduced to ashes.

Devastation.

That was the only word I could think of.

Absolute and total devastation.

It was clear the fire had jumped from one bank to the other, its embers carried on the wind and igniting both of the dry, tree-filled sides, those strong gusts of off-shore air growing the flames into the out-of-control complex blaze that was still burning west of town.

But not here.

Everything *here* had already burned.

So, I didn't stop driving across the bridge, didn't stop at the police cars, just began to swerve around them.

Except, then Frank, the sheriff, was standing there.

Exhaustion was written into the lines of his face, his uniform wrinkled and soot covered.

And he was at the front of my car, hands on the hood, and leaving no space for me to get by.

Unless I wanted to run him over.

Which was a thought that crossed my mind, I couldn't lie.

But while I was an asshole, I wasn't one who would commit vehicular homicide.

Plus, I was an asshole who might need Frank's assistance. Crushing him beneath my car probably wouldn't endear me to him, least of all get him to help me.

I threw the transmission into park but left the engine running as I pushed out the driver's side.

"I can't let you pass, Axel," he said before both of my feet hit the asphalt.

I shook my head. "I need to get to Bailey."

Something crossed Frank's face that had my gut twisting, that barbed wire gouging through my middle, leaving me flayed open and bleeding.

"What?" I rasped.

Frank rubbed a weary hand over his face. "The fire—" He dropped his hand, eyes lifting to mine, but only for a second before he was staring out over my shoulder.

"What the fuck, Frank?" I snapped, taking a jerking step toward him. "Just tell me."

"It started on her property," Frank said softly. "The whole fire did. And it spread fucking fast. So fast," he added, still quiet, so fucking quiet I had to strain to hear his words, "that we couldn't get help out there in time. Everything on Russet Ranch is gone— the house, the barn, the cattle, maybe there are a few head that managed to get away. But her other animals? No sign of them. And Bailey—"

My pulse had begun pounding so loudly in my ears that I couldn't hear the rest of what he was saying.

Everyone on Russet Ranch is gone.

Bailey—

Bailey was...what?

She couldn't be gone.

She couldn't be.

But Frank was still talking, and some distant part of my brain was processing that the sheriff had been out there, that he'd born witness, had seen the entire collection of ranches was gone.

That they'd already found more than one burned body.

Fuck.

Fuck.

It had to be a mistake. The flicker of hope was still alive and well in my chest.

She *had* to be okay.

I just needed to find her.

"I'm sorry, Axel," Frank choked out. "I just don't see how she could have survived that."

Those words came in crystal clear through the buzzing in my ears, my mind, slicing through the fog that I'd managed to cling to.

And it tore the fight right out of me.

My legs buckled and I barely felt the pain as my knees cracked against the asphalt. Skin broke, blood was a hot rush soaking into my jeans.

I felt a hand land on my shoulder, the rest of Frank's words fading away again.

Gone.

Gone.

My body was free of physical pain, too far gone to feel it. But that was only because the internal agony was too much, too over-whelming, too suffocating. The barbed wire grew and knotted, slicing my insides into ribbons, leaving me bleeding, the fluid choking me, filling my lungs, making it so I couldn't—

"It'll be okay, son."

How would it be okay?

I wanted to rail at him, to get back in my car and run over the man who was trying to smother the flickering bit of hope, who *was* smothering it. I wanted to toss him over the bridge, to punch and kick and slam him into the roadway until he didn't resemble a man, until he was a pile of flesh, resembling the useless piece of shit he was.

Fair? No.

But my person—*my person*—was out there and she w-was—

"We'll figure it out," Frank said and I wasn't so far gone as to miss the regret in his voice, the emotion turning it thick and rasping.

But I didn't care.

Because figure *what* out?

How to bring the woman I loved back from the dead?

How to fill in the hole in my heart, my soul, my life?

How—

I staggered to my feet, the physical pain finally slicing through the haze in my mind, sending the bone deep ache into my knees, up through my legs.

But it was still nothing compared to the pain *inside*.

"I need to get through," I said, trying to shove past him. I needed to see, needed to get to the ranch and—

The hand returned to my shoulder. "I can't let you through, son. I can't."

Fuck it.

I was going to run Frank over.

Yanking out of his hold, I spun back to my car then reached for the handle on the driver's side door.

But a flicker on the far bank caught my focus.

A flash of white.

The hand returned. "Axel—"

I shook it off, pointed to the opposite bank of the river. "What's that?"

"Axel—"

"*Frank*," I said. "*What's* that?"

Frank shut up, moved to my side. "What—?" I pointed again and he leaned forward, as though that would help him see better. "What *is* that?"

I didn't know, but I was already hopping over the end of the bridge where it met the bank on this side of the river and running down the hill, sprinting for the water, moving across it and—

The speck of white was moving down the bank, growing larger, coming into focus.

Then I was finally close enough to see it for what it was.

Picard.

FIVE

BAILEY

One second, I was tugging on Picard's harness and the next, I was sliding down that hill a second time, knocked there by my pet steer.

He hadn't meant it, I knew.

He was panicked by the roar of the flames that were too fucking close again.

But him panicking and trying to get away, to abruptly move down that hill because the fire sounded like it was moving in behind us again meant that he'd stumbled over me as I fell, as I slid through rocks and leaves and pine needles and dirt.

Worse was that when Picard started running forward and down, he didn't miss *me*.

I cursed, covering my head, curling up trying not to get trampled.

One of his hooves—carrying his three hundred and something pounds of steer—stepped on my thigh.

White hot pain seared through my leg. It was lightning down

through my toes, electricity shooting up to my hip, my spine, my shoulders and neck. Blood soaked into my back, making my T-shirt stick to my skin, and my arms and palms were scraped to shit, but I still tried to get up, still tried to move.

I *had* to keep moving.

Groaning, I managed to roll over, to get onto my hands and knees.

Except, I couldn't push to my feet. The leg that Picard had stepped on wasn't working right—maybe a bone was broken or perhaps the nerves just were shot from the sudden impact. I didn't know.

All I *did* know?

I needed to get the fuck out of there.

The fire...it was too damned close.

Spock whined when I began crawling, staying at my side, nudging my jaw with his cold nose.

It was no longer wet, which concerned me, especially considering how thirsty I was, but I couldn't do anything about it, not at that moment anyway.

Right then, I needed to keep moving forward.

So that was what I did.

"Picard!" I called when he didn't stop, but he disappeared ahead of us, lost from view in the brush, too panicked to heed my cries.

It hurt my heart, fucking hurt like *hell* to let him go. But I had to. The rumble was growing behind me, and I had Spock and Data and myself, for that matter, to worry about. "Move, Bay," I whispered. "Just keep moving."

So I did, clicking my tongue and thankful that Data trusted me enough that she started following me.

I knew I should ride her, but that would mean making it all the way up onto her back, and I didn't think that was possible for me at this point. Maybe if I found a rock I could climb on top of or an edge of the trail I could heave myself up onto, it might be possible to crawl onto her back, but here, *now*, it wasn't happening.

I barely had the strength to keep going.

But I did, rocks digging into my palms, slicing through my skin, and between my hands and my legs and my back, I worried I was bleeding so much that I didn't think it was possible for my body to lose any more blood, worried that I'd lost so much I was going to pass out and the flames were going to come for me.

Were going to get me.

"No," I whispered. I wouldn't let it.

Except, each foot I gained got harder, that constant drain of blood making my body grow weaker.

I embraced that fucking fish from *Finding Nemo*, except instead of swimming, it was crawling.

Just keep crawling.

Just keep crawling.

I did.

Somehow, I did just that. Continued moving, clicking my tongue, coaxing Data forward occasionally, but she and Spock weren't leaving my side and that fact made my eyes prickle with tears that couldn't actually form.

I was too dehydrated.

So the tears didn't come, but I continued moving down that steep trail, continuing hauling myself forward, and Spock and Data were right beside me.

Spock nudged me, that cool, dry nose hitting a sore spot—and truthfully there weren't really any spots on my body that weren't sore—but it still hurt, causing me to hiss out a breath, but when he nudged me again, I blinked, realized that I'd somehow stopped, even despite all of my *Just keep crawling.*

I was too weak.

I needed to rest, just for a little while.

But Spock kept nudging me and kept nudging me, even though I tried to bat him away.

That was when I realized the noise had grown, the flames were closer.

A bark. A sharp nudge.

I opened my eyes and there was a rock. A rock that I could clamber on top of. A rock that would get me high enough that if I could just get to the *fucking* top of it.

Spock barked again.

"Okay, okay," I whispered. "Yes, I know."

I pushed up onto my good leg, dug my hands into a crevice of the huge granite boulder and heaved.

My other leg got beneath me, held long enough that I managed to make it halfway up.

Cursing, grunting, groaning, *begging*, I did all of that.

But eventually I made it to the flat top of the rock.

Spock barked, encouraging me as I sank onto my bottom. "Yeah, boy. I know," I said again. "Come here, Data."

My horse, my friend, my best girl, shifted so that she was right next to the boulder.

A breath, sucking in my strength, holding tight to it.

Then I shifted enough to drop my bad leg over her back, to push with my good one, to...

I pushed too hard, nearly flew over to the other side.

"Fuck," I hissed, managing to grip Data's mane, to stop myself from toppling to the ground. I was lightheaded, my lungs on fire, my entire body one raw, exposed nerve.

But I was on Data's back.

Crackling was in the air, branches and tree trunks catching fire. The temperature increased, causing sweat to drip down my spine, my chest, burning and stinging all along the salty tracks.

The smoke was coming back, clogging my nose and mouth and lungs.

We *had* to go.

I clicked my tongue.

Data started moving.

I focused on keeping my seat, on making sure that Spock was staying next to us.

And then all my focus turned to staying conscious.

And...I didn't succeed.

Six

AXEL

I ran toward the white and brown cow. Bull. Steer. Whatever the fuck the non-milk producing, ball-less variety of cattle was supposed to be called. Bailey had corrected me more than once, but to me he was a cow.

Brown and white with four legs and a tail and big, cow eyes and hooves.

A *cow*.

Who was sprinting down the hill now, hooves sliding, big body moving fast.

Fuck.

Too fast.

He was going to slip and fall and break something, and I didn't know cows or steers or whatever well at all, but I didn't think him breaking a leg was going to end well.

My feet splashed through the water, skidding on the slippery rocks, but I'd grown up on skates, so I moved with the skid, slid across the slick stones and then I was on the other side of the water, up onto the rocky bank and then moving across the sandy shore.

Crashing in my ears, rocks skittering down toward me, and then Picard was there, covered in soot and ash, small burns all his sides, blood streaked across his face to create a ghoulish mask.

He was wearing his halter, a rope dangling from its end.

"Hey, buddy," I said gently, reaching out and taking the end of the rope, pulling it, slowing him down, harder now because he had to weigh a good three or four hundred pounds and he was scared, but I did manage to turn him before we both ended up in the water, though he was still dragging me forward.

And then Frank was there beside me, helping me haul Picard to a halt.

"Easy, buddy," I said again and, finally, Picard stopped fighting me, stopped lurching against the harness. He froze, sides heaving, snot and blood and drool coming out of his mouth and nose. But he was there and he was okay.

So Bailey must—

I dropped the length of rope I'd grabbed on to. "Get him up the other side." I turned for the hill Picard had sprinted down.

"What are you doing?" Frank asked.

"Bailey might be up there."

Frank grabbed my arm. "You can't—"

"He's harnessed," I snapped. "That means Bailey got out. Got out," I said sharply, talking over him when he opened his mouth to reply, "soon enough to get him harnessed and off the ranch."

Frank's brows dragged together, but thankfully, he shut up.

"I'm going," I said. "She's got to be close."

The vee between the sheriff's brows deepened and unfortunately, he began talking again. "Axel, that's not—"

I ran out of patience.

"Get him up the bank. At least save *hi*—" I snapped my teeth together, not willing, not able to have this conversation. "Go," I ordered.

And then I was done talking.

I was sprinting up the hill, feet sliding on the loose earth, hands gripping the burned branches to haul myself up the extra slippery parts.

Lungs burning from smoke, from exertion. Legs shaking but not giving out.

Then I was in amongst the charred trees, eyes searching for a glimpse of shining brown hair, ears listening hard for any sound of movement.

Nothing.

All quiet.

Not even the whisper of the wind.

My heart sank, but I kept moving, kept making my way up the trail, up through the trees, until I'd reached the precipice...and saw nothing but...

Nothing.

Trees turned to cinder.

The hillsides bare.

My disappointment was acute, biting and sharp and leaving me bleeding out on the remains of the forest floor.

But still I looked, still I searched, that flicker of hope in my heart, my belly guttering, fading, threatening to go out. Somehow, I managed to keep it aflame, mostly because I kept walking, kept moving forward, kept *looking*.

Picard had come down the bank, had come from this direction.

The ranch wasn't all that close, at least ten miles north, but that wasn't a straight path. The hills followed the curves of the river, and the fire had burned along both sides at various stretches. For Picard to be *here*, to be here now...it meant he'd—*they'd*—taken a circuitous path from the ranch.

They'd taken a circuitous path.

I inhaled, that flicker blooming anew.

Then I started walking again.

Down through the trees, the loose dirt kicked up by my shoes, creating a cloud of dust that choked almost as much as the smoke. It was thick. That was why I couldn't see her.

That was why she wasn't immediately visible—the visibility sucked. How could I see her through it?

So I just needed to keep moving, to keep searching.

Up the next hill, beyond the parking lot for the river trail. Then I was climbing my way through patches of random green trees, completely unburned, completely untouched by the devastation. Patches that gave me hope, that fed the flicker in my belly.

If these weren't destroyed then they—

Then she was okay.

Then she was *okay.*

I inhaled, the air tighter here, not as much oxygen available for my lungs, for my mind. The doubts creeping in all over again, wondering how in the fuck she could survive in this, how she could have survived *any* of this.

"Fuck," I whispered, fingers digging into a tree trunk that was still hot from being burned. "*Fuck.*"

I should go back, should make sure the Picard—

A rustle.

It had been so quiet, so silent. No noise except for the sound of my footsteps, the rasp of my breathing, the pounding of my pulse in my ears.

Except for that rustle.

I froze listening harder.

Hearing it again.

"Bailey!" I shouted.

It was just torn out of me, so loud, so abrupt that I shocked the shit out of myself, nearly tripped as I started running.

"Bailey!" I yelled again, not surprised this time.

Determined.

A bark.

A *bark.*

That hope growing, bursting outward.

"Spock!" I shouted, speeding forward, tripping and landing hard on my knees again, the cuts from the bridge stinging, but I just pushed up to my feet again, just started running again, just—

A flash of dirty fur, white parts dyed gray and brown from the smoke and dust.

A yip of excitement.

A dog crashing into me, nearly taking me off my feet again. I scooped him up, held his wriggling body close. His tongue hit my cheek and it was dry, so dry that I knew he needed help.

But he lived his life glued to Bailey's side. I knew he wouldn't leave her.

And just as I had that thought, as I *knew* that she had to be close, I looked up and saw chestnut fur.

It was grayed out. It was muted and stained.

But it was chestnut-colored.

It was *Data's*.

I inhaled sharply, coughing on the ash, and setting Spock down and then I was moving again, sprinting now.

Because I could see there was a harness similar to Picard's over Data's nose. No saddle, no stirrups down her naked side.

No...Bailey.

I cursed, knees threatening to give way again.

But I had to see, had to get closer.

And when I did, when I got to Data, stroked her nose and watched her panic-filled eyes settle slightly, I saw I was right.

No saddle.

No Bailey.

No—

Spock barked again, bumping my legs as he ran back in the direction from where he and Data had just come, drawing my gaze after him.

My mouth parted to call him back.

Then he barked again.

And every cell in my body went ramrod still.

Brown hair coated with dirt and ash.

A glimpse of exposed skin that I'd kissed my way across, that had felt like silk beneath my lips, smelled like apples and horses and hay.

I'd told her once that she smelled like shit, so fucking scared of what was in my heart and head, so fucking scared of feeling like *this* —like I'd lost her, like I was clinging to hope that she was still breathing—that I'd done every fucking *thing* to keep her from getting close.

She'd gotten in anyway.

And now...she was going to destroy me.

Bracing myself, I approached the unmoving body of the woman I loved.

SEVEN

BAILEY

My eyelids hurt.

Everything hurt.

But the part that stood out the most was the fact that my eyelids hurt so much I couldn't even stand to open them.

And I was trying to open them because I'd figured out that I wasn't in that burned forest, that the flames weren't coming for me.

My skin was burning. My lungs ached. My leg—there was a deep, radiating sort of bone-deep pain. But my eyelids. *God*. They hurt so fucking much and all I wanted to do was to open them, to see where I was.

"Wake up, buttercup. Pl-please just wake up."

The voice was fuzzy, slow to penetrate.

But then it did, and my lids flew open. It *hurt*...but not as much as seeing the look on Axel's face.

The area beneath his eyes was bruised with dark circles. His skin was deathly pale. But it was the agony etched into his expression as his stare left my body and drifted up to stare at the wall over my head that eclipsed any of the pain currently present in my body.

"Axel," I whispered.

Too quiet.

My voice gone.

But I tried to clear my throat, to get it to be loud enough for him to hear me, needing him to know I was here, I was okay.

"Axel," I whispered again.

His head snapped back toward me, eyes going wide, pain replaced with shock and, for now, that was enough.

"Hi," I whispered.

He collapsed.

That was the only way I could think to describe what happened to his body—it was as though all of the inner struts, the support structure that was keeping him together just totally collapsed. His body folded forward, going limp, his head dropping to my belly, his arms wrapping around my middle, squeezing, but doing it gently.

So, so gently.

And then his back began to shake, his tears soaking through the blanket, through the hospital gown I was wearing.

Which was the first time that I realized I was in a hospital.

I was safe.

Though, I supposed, I had known that I was out of harm's way the moment I'd heard Axel's voice.

He was my safe space. He was my lodestone, my guiding star in a midnight sky.

So, I just lifted a hand, smoothed it down his shaking back, ignoring the slight tug of the IV in my hand, and waited for him to finish.

When he did, when he lifted his head and I caught sight of those reddened eyes, the pain radiated right through my veins, more intense than the flames bearing down on me. "Picard—" I began, voice cracking.

"He's okay," Axel murmured, gently smoothing back my hair. "He's the reason I found you. Data and Spock, too. They're all fine. Olivia and Cole picked them up, had their vet check them out, and then took them to their ranch. They can stay there as long as we need."

Relief was a cool drink of water after the hours of everything being so hot and dry and *parched*. I knew that Axel's agent and her former hockey playing, now charity ranch owning husband would take care of them. Just like I knew—

I laced our fingers together, held his gaze. "I knew you'd find me."

My certainty seemed to shoot like electricity through him, through his expression, down through his body, taking it statue still, turning it rigid. Then everything seemed to relax in him and he brushed my hair back again, telling me about Picard flying down the riverbank, hearing Spock, spotting Data, and then finding me, seemingly having finally fallen from Data's back.

How I'd managed to stay atop her to make my way through the miles between where Picard had spooked and run off and where Axel had found me, was a miracle in and of itself. I couldn't be certain precisely how many miles that was, but I did know that it was more than a few.

I'd been thoroughly lost in those woods.

And Data and Spock had gotten me out—and Picard, even though he'd run off, had helped with the rescue just as much.

Axel touched my cheek. "I love you."

Those words were electricity through *me*.

And all that had happened was pushed away for the moment. Because then I *remembered* what had happened before the fire. What I'd done. What—

"The game," I blurted. "I'm so sorry I did that—"

A shake of his head, his thumb gently rubbing over my skin. "It doesn't matter."

It *did* matter. It mattered to me a whole hell of a lot.

I was a fuck-up. I—

Guilt seeped into my skin, into my bones.

I'd hurt him and—

"Oh, my God!" I shot up—or partway, anyway—because my sudden jerk up to sitting sent waves of pain ricocheting through my body. Monitors began beeping, my heart rate increasing, but I couldn't focus on that, couldn't focus on anything except trying to get my breath back, on trying to not let the wave of black pain take me under again. "Fuck," I hissed, dropping back to the hospital bed...and aggravating all of those hurts all over again.

God. That *hurt*.

"Bruised ribs," Axel murmured, gently stroking my forehead. "Broken leg, second degree burns on your arms, contusions and bruising and cuts on your back, several of which required stitches. They also treated you for severe smoke inhalation."

I wanted to tell him not to touch me, to back the fuck up and let me breathe.

It was hard enough to suck in air, even with the oxygen mask strapped to my face, and the agony coursing through my body made every nerve so fucking raw that I could barely think.

But the careful recitation had reached my brain, even through the haze of pain.

And it tempered my...well, it tempered my temper.

So I stayed still on the bed, breathed, let him touch me, waited until the hurt faded to a more reasonable level before I opened my eyes again.

"The game. When is the final game?" I asked the question I'd been working up to before I'd set off a whole cascade of pain through my body.

For a second, he wasn't computing what I was asking, but then it seemed as though he did because his body stilled and he started shaking his head, eyes drifting away from mine. "I'm going to get the nurse, let her know that you're awake, see if she can give you something for the pain."

He stood up, chair skidding back.

"Axel."

Rounded the end of my bed.

"*Axel.*"

He stopped.

Wouldn't look at me.

"I'll get the nurse," he said again, starting forward.

My gut clenched, the monitors going crazy again, my heart racing again. Then I pulled out the big guns. "Don't leave me."

That stopped him.

But it didn't bring him closer, didn't unlock his face, didn't bring him to my side.

"Axel, honey, please," I said, lifting my hand.

Finally, he came back, taking my hand in his. "You're hurting," he murmured.

"So are you," I whispered.

A breath.

"Did you miss it?" I asked. Because of me? Did he miss game seven, miss his chance to win a Cup because of me? Remorse and guilt tangling through me, sinking barbs into my belly. And sinking them deeper when a worse notion entered my mind.

Had they lost?

Because of me? Because of the fire? Because Axel was here, had been in River's Bend searching for me? Had they lost because I'd needed him, but they'd needed him too?

"Calm down, buttercup," he murmured. "Just breathe."

"It's my fault."

A shake of his head. "No, honey. It's not your fault. The game is tomorrow."

My eyes went to the clock, saw it was almost midnight. "You need to go," I said. "You need to go *right now*."

EIGHT

AXEL

She had lost her ever loving mind if she thought I was going to leave her.

Wasn't going to fucking happen.

Not for hockey.

Not for anything.

I'd nearly lost her. I was playing Superglue with her for the rest of her fucking life.

"You *need* to go," she repeated.

"I'm not leaving you." I didn't say anything else. I didn't need to. It was as simple as that.

Argument in her eyes, frustration in her frame. And pain. Too much pain. I needed to get the nurse, needed to get her some more meds.

Maybe they'd make her drowsy enough that she'd lose that argument, would close her eyes and rest. Now that I knew she'd wake up, that she was okay, every part of me wanted to demand that she rest, that she recover and heal.

But surprisingly, the argument faded from her expression,

from her pretty brown eyes. Instead, she relaxed further into her pillow and turned her head toward me. "Where are we?" I asked.

"Sacramento," he said, "The trauma team brought you here."

She nodded.

I took her hand again, found myself saying, probably stupidly, "The team is fine. They don't need me."

Her eyes flared, lips pressing flat beneath the oxygen mask. "They *need* you."

They didn't.

They'd won Cups before. They could do it now.

And that wasn't me being all self-deprecating. It was fact. The San Francisco Gold were a force in the league, and they knew how to battle back—case in point the game two days before where they'd been down, where they'd faced elimination and the series being over without winning it all.

They'd regrouped, made a comeback.

Of course, a lot of that had to do with the woman in this bed, for her managing to get a message to me that had gotten my head straight. And yeah, I'd helped with that comeback, had pulled my weight. But we were a team. It was more than just me on the roster. And maybe it made me an asshole, but someone else could step up and shoulder that burden.

Bailey was more important.

Than *anything*.

Even winning it all.

"Axel, you need to go."

My eyes narrowed. "I'm not leaving you," I growled. "So just get that fucking idea out of your mind."

"The game tomorrow isn't a normal one," she said. "It's important. It's a once in a lifetime game. It's a dream—*your* dream —and you know it."

I *did* know it.

I'd wanted to hoist the Cup from the moment I'd first seen my heroes doing in on TV as a kid. That I'd played in the finals at all was a fucking momentous occasion, that we were one game away from winning it all was even bigger.

Plenty of players never got that opportunity.

That *I'd* made it was something special. I—a fuck-up who'd nearly dive-bombed my own career and made it to where I was by sheer dumb luck (and yes, the part of me that was growing and maturing knew that it had also been via hard work)—*done* it.

And I might never get another chance.

So, I wasn't taking missing that game lightly.

But I needed to be here, be with the woman I loved. No fucking *game* was more important than what I had with her.

"It is a dream," I admitted, "but it pales in the face of the dream of you."

She inhaled sharply, and then again when she winced from the sharpness of her previous breath.

"You should rest," I told her.

Her skin was still so pale. Her body broken. Her eyelids growing heavy, even after the small amount of time that she'd been awake.

"Billie Rose?" she asked instead of letting them slid closed, instead of allowing herself to drift off.

"She's okay. I saw her in one of the shelters, along with Dessie and most of the town. Because of you," I added, smoothing my knuckles along her cheek. "Billie got your call and activated the town's emergency system. Joel and Ryan and the rest of the guys helped evacuate almost everyone since they were all downtown together watching the game."

That was the only reason the casualties were so low when the destruction was so vast.

Many had left cars behind, packing the biggest ones full of residents—people only returning to their homes for pets, for kids.

All of it had meant less cars on the road, less traffic.

Because when they'd heard from Bailey, seen how quickly the fire had been moving, Billie Rose—mayor of River's Bend and

Bailey's aunt (who was somehow only two years older because, well...small towns)—had used her militant planning skills for good. I should have known she'd been prepared, she was positively obsessed with planning and preparation.

Having done so for an emergency was right in her wheelhouse.

Bailey's warning, Billie Rose's preparation, the residents' knowledge of the plan and willingness to follow it all meant that the casualties had been minimal.

And all from Bailey's end of town.

Which was why I was here, holding her hand, not leaving her after she'd nearly left this fucking planet, after she'd nearly left *me*.

I knew there would be time for her to find out that all of her neighbors had died, that her herd might be completely lost...there would be plenty of time for loss later. Right now, I was going to focus on the fact that she was still here.

She nodded, lids growing heavy. "I'm glad."

"Rest now, buttercup," I murmured. "I'll get the nurse and come right back."

Another nod, this one punctuated by a yawn. "Okay."

Her eyes closed.

I rose, pressed a kiss to her forehead, stood up again, and this time wasn't pulled back to her beside—or at least, not before I managed to get the nurses attention and let her know that she'd woken up and was hurt.

I stepped out into the hall when asked, barely able to hear Bailey's sleepy voice as she answered the questions the nurse—and then the doctor, when she slipped into the room— asked. But her voice was there, and it soothed the razor's edge of need slicing at me to go to her, to hold her hand and touch her and convince myself that she was safe and alive and *here*.

The doctor and nurse were in there for long enough for my nerves to prickle, and by the time they let me back in, my heart was beating hard enough for my knees to shake as I moved over to her.

She was awake. Barely.

But the oxygen mask was gone, the lines of strain that had been etched into her face were fading.

"They give you some pain meds?" I asked.

"Yeah, honey," she said, lifting her hand.

I tugged the chair close to her bedside again, took her hand, lacing my fingers through hers. "Good." Bending, I kissed her knuckles. "You should rest now."

I would just sit here and watch her.

Creepy, yes.

But also, I needed to remind myself that she was alive and safe, to keep reminding myself. To—

She tugged lightly and I shifted my gaze from our interlaced hands up to her face. "Lay next to me?" she asked.

"No—"

"If you won't go," she said softly, her tone cutting right through me, "then at least hold me." Another tug when I looked away, drawing my eyes to hers again. "Let me have this," she whispered. "Let me know that you're resting too. Let me take care of you so that I can rest easy."

I glanced toward the far side of the room, nodded. "I can sleep on the cot."

I didn't want to jostle her leg, to hurt her, to—

"With me," she whispered and I opened my mouth to argue further, but then she said, "Please, honey."

And denial was an impossibility.

Denying her *anything* wasn't in my DNA.

So, I carefully helped her shift enough so that I could crawl in on her uninjured side. Then, just as carefully, I took her in my arms.

Her breathing evened out.

Sleep took her under.

And then I was slipping down right beside her.

NINE

BAILEY

He wasn't going to go.

He wasn't.

He could be a stubborn asshole when he really put his mind to it.

And his mind was set. S.E.T. Set.

But I hadn't survived a wildfire—hadn't survived what I'd just survived only to be responsible for imploding Axel's dream.

So, I just had to prove to him that I could be sneakier.

My groundwork had been laid hours before, when the doctor had come in to examine me. It continued now, with him resting beside me, resting up for the game of his life.

It would continue into the morning.

The doctor was coming back at the end of her shift, would be checking on my vitals, making sure my lungs were strong enough to be...

Discharged.

My leg would be a pain in the ass. My ribs even more so.

Even now with the morphine in my system, the edge of all my injuries was razor sharp just beyond my focus, a hazy throb.

Tolerable.

But there.

Maybe less tolerable when the morphine wore off.

But I would manage. I always did.

And anyway, I could manage it for this.

I *would* manage it for Axel.

Next step of that?

Sleeping enough so that I would have the strength to fight him when he heard about my plan.

————

"Absolutely fucking *not!*"

Okay, so I might need more than strength to fight Axel on this.

I might need handcuffs and several big, broody hockey players and maybe a security specialist.

Luckily, I had several men who fit those categories on hand, having called them while Axel slept deeply. They were standing out in the hall—all except Joel, who was standing in the doorway, his face pointed in my direction, brows lifted in question.

I nodded and he came into the room.

"Axel, man," he muttered. "Take a breath."

"She is *not* leaving this fucking hospital bed," Axel snapped, shoving a hand through his hair. "She almost died an-and—" Breaking off, he pressed both of his fists to his eyes, spinning away from me, his back as stiff as a board.

Joel moved over to him, leaning close, talking quietly.

The doctor squeezed my shoulder lightly. "I'll get the paperwork going, and make sure that referral for the respiratory specialist is on it. Any difficulty breathing, you don't mess around. You go to the ED."

I nodded. "I will."

Another squeeze and then she pushed in the keyboard tray connected to the computer that she'd been logging everything and slipped out of the room.

Axel still had his back to me, Joel at his side. Ryan slipped inside the room when the doctor left, nodding at me and moving over to the pair.

I hoped they'd get through where I couldn't.

I inhaled, released it slowly.

It didn't feel normal, my lungs were going to take a while to heal, but it didn't feel like it had when I'd been in the trees, in the smoke, in the ash. They weren't tight, didn't make me feel like I was suffocating, like I couldn't pull in enough air. The burns on my arms hurt, my leg was a constant ache. Unfortunately, I knew from past experience that my ribs were going to give me trouble for a good long while, and my back felt beyond tender, like even the sheet pressing into it was too much sensation.

But I was alive.

I was okay.

I was getting the fuck out of here.

"Fuck, man," Axel snapped. "It doesn't matter how many different ways you say it, you're not going to convince me that it's a good idea for her to leave that bed." He spun, his gorgeous face a harsh contrast of lines and furrows, of twitching muscles and a beard growing out of control. "You're not leaving that"—he jabbed a finger in my direction"—*bed.*"

I loved this man.

I understood that he must have been out of his mind with worry.

But I was a grown woman. I'd been taking care of myself for a long, long time. Hell, if I was really thinking up about my fucked-up past and my childhood, the truth was that I'd been taking care of myself for almost my entire life. Add in a dash of my abusive ex, Colt—who'd broken me down, who'd controlled me, who'd hit and kicked and punched me—and I wasn't going to roll over and let someone make decisions for me.

Yes, I loved him.

Yes, I could grant him some patience, dish out plenty of understanding.

But that patience and understand wasn't unending.

And—spoiler alert—I was getting to the end of it.

Very quickly.

Taking a breath before I could snap back at him, I gripped tight to my restraint, said quietly, "Don't tell me what I can or can't do."

His blue eyes were filled with sparks of anger, with sparks of fire, with sparks that sent a chill down my spine because it took me right back to those moments on the ranch—scrambling to reach Billie Rose and Dessie, to reach Tommy and Hank and Eli as I hooked up my trailer, as I struggled to get Picard and Data harnessed, to get Spock in the truck and to get on the road.

My pulse sped on the monitor, the rapid *beep-beeping* drawing Axel's focus, drawing *everyone's* focus.

Another breath.

Deliberate breathing.

Focused inhales and exhales.

The beeping slowed.

I held his gaze. "I'm going to that game, honey."

His mouth opened—

Billie Rose strode into the room. She looked at Axel, at me, probably understanding all that was going down in that one glimpse, taking that single reading of the room, even though her clothes were dirty and soot-stained and wrinkled. She had ash on her cheeks, dark circles beneath her eyes, and looked like she hadn't rested since the fire had broken out.

She probably *hadn't*.

And now she was here. Safe.

A bit of tension—tension I hadn't even realized that I'd been holding on to—slid from me.

My aunt was one of the few people I could trust wholeheartedly, and she was okay.

My eyes burned and not from fucking smoke for once.

I glanced at my hand—now free of the IV, thanks to a helpful nurse—and concentrated on not losing my shit.

Later, I could freak the fuck out, could process all the fear and grief that was swirling in my mind.

Right now—*today, tonight*—I needed to hold on to my strength.

For Axel.

"Why's big, hot, and hockey glowering?" she asked chipperly.

"I'm being discharged," I told her.

Billie smiled. "That's a good thing."

"She thinks she's going to Game Seven tonight," Axel gritted out.

My aunt's gaze had swung toward Axel at his announcement. Now it swung back to connect with mine, her brows lifting in silent query.

I dragged mine together, making a silent point.

I *was going* to the fucking game...and more importantly, *Axel* was going.

A flex of her brows. Was I sure?

Mine drawing together even more tightly. Yes, I was fucking *sure*.

A slight nod and then she was turning back to Axel. "So," she said in her typical Billie Rose Voice (determined, authoritative, not to be trifled with), "are you taking her? Or am I?"

Fury on his face.

A muscle twitching in his cheek.

But it was my aunt speaking. It was Billie Rose and she had that magical ability to get everything to work out, to get everyone to behave.

To get my stubborn man to give in, even when it was in regard to something as important to him as my safety.

Because after a long silence—taut and furious—Axel gritted out, "*I'm* fucking taking her."

I smiled.

He softened, crossing over to me, taking my hand.

But as he leaned down, brushed his lips over mine, murmured, "You so owe me," I caught a glimpse behind him.

A glimpse of Joel.

And he was looking...pensive. No, not *pensive*. His expression was gentle, almost that same sort of soft that Axel's had when he was looking at me.

But Joel's gaze wasn't pointed at my hospital bed.

It was fixed on Billie Rose.

TEN

AXEL

My focus was fucked.

I felt like I had to tell Coach that.

I owed it to the team. They should scratch me, bench me, get someone else who was more focused, more motivated.

My whole heart was several floors up, in the Family Suite, sitting on the couch, her leg propped up with pillows.

I'd gotten her settled upstairs, Mandy—the head athletic trainer for the team—having taken over from Billie Rose, who'd needed to get back to River's Bend, back to her town, her people.

The fire was still burning, still out of control, still consuming acres of land and houses by the second.

A fucking monster.

A *complex*, not just a fire.

But none of the neighboring towns were faring as bad as River's Bend had. The firefighters had time to dig in, to set up fire lines, to protect them.

Sighing, I tried to push that from my head, but it was pounding and I was exhausted.

Two more reasons to tell Coach I couldn't play.

Along with the fact that I'd barely slept. And my body was beat up. Plus, my legs—hell, I wasn't sure if they could hold me.

"She's okay."

I glanced up, not realizing that I'd just been sitting there while everyone else was getting dressed, just sitting there staring at my hands, *sitting* there being completely useless.

Mandy, the team's head trainer and the person who was supposed to be looking after my woman, was crouched in front of me.

Fuck.

My body immediately tensed with concern. "Bailey—"

"Is with Stefan and Mia and Charlie." A smile. "And the rest of the crew. They're not going to let her so much as lift a finger." She held up her cell. "And they know to call me if there's any issue, big or small. Not just Bailey," she added at was no doubt the obvious protest welling up on my face. "*All* of them," she told me. "And I'll be checking on her." She passed over some smelling salts. "Sniff. Breathe. Clear your mind. I've got her."

"I should—"

"Be down here, doing your job," Mandy said. "Just like she ordered *me* to do. Make her proud," she whispered. "Don't make her carry the weight of this game—whatever the outcome—on her shoulders."

I stilled.

And for the first time I understood exactly why Bailey was pushing this.

My legs *were* shit. I *was* exhausted—both from the long ass season and the events of the last couple of days.

But I'd worked my ass off for this.

Win or lose, it didn't compare to Bailey, to what I felt for her.

I would give my chance to hoist that Cup up in an instant and have absolutely no regrets.

But *she'd* have them, and now I had a choice—allow those regrets to settle on her shoulders, to fester, to make her carry something else, something she damned well shouldn't have to. Or to make a different choice.

It was *no* choice.

I couldn't do that to her.

I *wouldn't*.

I gripped the smelling salts.

I inhaled and immediately felt my mind grow clear, getting that sharp jolt of alertness so many of my teammates avowed that the salts gave them. Supposedly, they expanded the blood vessels, allowed a person to draw in more oxygen. That said, I still wasn't sure if it was something that actually worked.

But, in that moment, I didn't care.

Between Mandy's words and the smelling salts I was finally thinking clearly.

I was finally ready.

"We got her," Mandy said softly. "And we've got you, okay?"

My heart—the formerly ice-cold, almost completely dead organ, at least until Bailey had entered my life—convulsed. Feelings. Too many of them, and each one of them was too fucking big.

But I wouldn't go back. I was too selfish to give them up—any of them—the feelings, the people, the love in my sappy fucking heart.

"Okay," I whispered.

Mandy squeezed my knee, stood, and left the room.

And that was when I finally processed my teammates' mood— they were all deliberately getting dressed, all completely focused on prepping for the game. I could see that in the way they moved, in the lack of chatter and jokes and back talk.

But that wasn't *us*.

Yeah, we played hockey, and did it intensely, because it was our fucking job.

But we weren't this quiet, tense locker room, everyone afraid to speak, to disturb the hushed atmosphere that had descended.

We were laughter and shit-giving.

We were tossing sock balls across the room, and then busting the other type of balls when someone didn't dodge fast enough.

We were leaving it all on the ice but coming back to *family* in the room.

I knew the hushed air, the quiet that had descended, was because they were thinking about me—and no, that wasn't ego talking. They were worried. They were focused. They wanted to bring this game home for me, for Bailey, for the community that was rooting for us and had now lost everything.

The stakes were high, about as high as they could be for us.

This wasn't life or death. We weren't firefighters out in the wilderness trying to save houses and lives and pets.

But it meant something.

Meant something *more* after everything that had happened.

Which was why I knew that I needed to pack away the fear, the tumult, and get my shit together. Which was *why*—and maybe to someone who hadn't spent the last months wouldn't understand why I did what I did next, but...hell, life didn't make sense sometimes, *hockey* didn't make sense sometimes. Pucks bounced off unseen chunks of ice, sending passes askew, causing a goal because it ricocheted off a skate or an ass or the butt end of a stick.

All of which was why I took the sock that was sitting on the bench next to me, rolled it into a ball—something I had lots of practice with, considering that my nickname—Balls—had unfortunately stuck.

Originating because of my excellent Harvest Festival fortune telling, a la the Fantastic Finnegano—and if *that*—me caressing a crystal ball, me wearing fucking *guy*liner as part of my costume—

didn't illustrate *exactly* how much I would do for Bailey and Billie Rose and River's Bend as a whole then I didn't know what would.

But right then I was taking advantage of the fact that the name Balls had stuck to put my...

I paused, knowing that my next thought was bad. *Really* bad.

I finished it anyway.

Because today I was about finishing things, finishing *this* thing, getting that motherfucking Cup.

So right then, I was going to take advantage of my nickname Balls and put my *balls* to use.

Heh.

"Brit?"

More than a little distracted, she glanced in my direction, but her focus wasn't on me, not really. "Yeah?"

I let the ball fly.

It sailed across the room, and truthfully, I expected her to catch it. Her reflexes were incredible, snagging hundred mile per hour shots out of midair, so a sock ball should be easy pickings.

But she didn't catch it.

The sock ball flew right through the air...

And beaned her directly in the middle of her forehead.

If I'd been my normal self, I think I might have fallen over because I'd be laughing too hard. As it was, I was too shocked to react.

I felt my eyes go wide.

Will, sitting beside me, turned to face me, expression an exhibit of shock.

Rome, on my other side, was less shocked. He started busting up laughing, nearly falling off the bench in the process.

And that was enough.

The laughter encompassed the room, ringing off the walls, a pin into a balloon of tension, suddenly releasing it...and leaving them...*them.*

Brit launched the sock back at me. I dodged. The shit-giving commenced. The laughter continued. The focus stayed, right on the edge, but it was that loose, Gold focus.

I got dressed.

I laughed.

I breathed.

I thanked fuck that we were in this position, in this *place,* in this moment.

Geared up, Brit crossed to me, thwapping me on the side of the head. "Balls?"

I waited for the payback, or maybe, for another, harder *thwack.* "Yeah?"

"Let's fucking go, yeah?"

My pulse began to speed up, and I nodded. "Let's fucking go."

ELEVEN

BAILEY

This was maybe one of the dumbest things I'd ever done.

But I was still glad I was doing it.

Even as the pain was creeping in past the painkillers, my leg a solid thrum of hurt, I wasn't going to give in.

I wasn't going to miss this.

"If you were mine, I'd paddle your ass."

Startled, I blinked up at Stefan. He was so gentle, so easy-going that the words coming out of *his* mouth surprised me. Though, I supposed they were tempered by the twinkle in his eyes. "I think that Brit would paddle *your* ass if she heard you say that."

"Damn right, she would." A flash of a smile. "But I like to keep my wife on her toes." A beat of quiet. "Otherwise, she's hell on wheels."

That made *me* want to smile. "I think she's hell on wheels, no matter how much you try to keep her on her toes."

He touched my cheek, eyes soft. "Yeah, she is." Then he held up the pain medicine bottle. "But I'd still make her take the pills her doctor prescribed."

"They make me sleepy," I protested. My plan was to try to make it through the game, to take it toward the end, so that I didn't miss anything.

"They also make you not hurt," he said. "And since I promised Mandy to take care of you and *she* promised Axel that we would *both* take care of you, I'm"—he shook the bottle, the pills rattling in the plastic container—"keeping you to your schedule."

I bit my lip.

"I'll keep you awake," he said, mouth turning up at the corners. "*If* our guys are playing so well and the game is so much of a blowout that you're dozing off." He winked. "Otherwise, I think this will be a live wire of a matchup and you'll be riding the adrenaline high late into the night."

A sigh. Then I stuck my hand out for the bottle. "Fine," I grumbled. "Give me the drugs."

He opened the lid, which was nice of him (then again, that was Stefan Barie, former captain and current hubby of the illustrious Brit Plantain), and handed me the container. I dutifully took my pills, which truthfully, hurt more than a little bit going down my poor, abused throat. Then I passed the bottle back. He screwed the lid back on, studied me closely. "They'll take this game," he said softly. "If only because Axel knows exactly what—" His eyes focused on me, intense and warm and...suddenly my pain wasn't as bad, and whether it was because Stefan was just so freaking nice or a placebo effect from me immediately taking the pills, I didn't know. All I *did* know was that when Stefan looked at me like that, when he gently squeezed my hand, when he said, "He—*they* know exactly what they're playing for," I felt better.

I felt good.

I felt like the world might end up okay.

"Good," he said, seemingly reading those thoughts as they drifted across my face. "Good."

———

I didn't like hockey.

I didn't *like* it.

In fact, I was deciding that I despised the sport, despising what it did to my man, to my friends, to the family I was slowly becoming part of.

It was brutal.

It was fast. *Too* fucking fast.

I was watching the game on the big screen TVs mounted to the wall of the Family Suite, knowing that while I might make it down the hall and to the luxury box where I could watch the game from a spot perched high above the rink, I wouldn't last long there. It was too cramped, too full of people, and I was too nervous, too on edge, too ready to jump with every crack of the stick on the ice, to wince with every brutal hit, to gnaw my nails down to their nubs.

At least here I had a sort of privacy.

Sort of because there were lots of people in this set of rooms.

But they were also jumping with every play and missed pass and shot on goal. They were wincing and biting their nails with each hit and good scoring chance on Brit. Basically, they were as riveted to the TVs as I was, and because I was taking up an entire couch—and the littles had been warned to keep their distance because of my leg (and burns and stitches)—I pretty much had a slice of the room to myself.

And Stefan.

But I was only somewhat aware of him.

Because I was spending the majority of my time hating this sport.

The Gold had gone up on the scoreboard quickly, Coop scoring a goal that even my non-hockey appreciative brain knew had been all sorts of pretty. But then, less than a minute later, the game had been tied up, the puck sailing in on an impossibly fast shot that I hadn't even *seen*.

It had taken me two replays to see it sail into the tiny sliver of space between Brit's head and shoulder.

Now it had been almost three full periods and the score was still tied one to one, and I was...

Hell.

I was freaking the fuck out.

Stefan was right.

I didn't need to worry in the least about the pain medicine putting me to sleep. I was so freaking alert, so attuned to every play, big or small, on the ice that I didn't think I'd be able to sleep ever again.

The pillow I'd crammed behind my head was making my neck ache, my leg was a constant thrum, my burns alternated between itching and hurting, but my mind was only distantly processing that because every bit of focus was on how much I *hated* hockey.

Mostly because I was watching the man I loved, the people I liked fight and bleed and *try* so freaking hard.

And I couldn't do anything to help them.

Ugh.

I hated it.

I hated hockey.

Yes, I knew I'd said that. But it bared repeating.

"I feel exactly the same."

Blinking, I glanced up at Stefan. He was resting a hip against the back of the couch I was laying on. He'd been alternating between that position and pacing, though he'd spent most of his time pacing.

"What?" I asked.

"I hate being up here," the former captain of the team playing several stories below muttered. "It never gets easier, the ache never goes away." He sighed, shoved a hand through his hair. "I know I had my time, and I don't regret retiring, but *fuck* do I hate being up here while they're battling down there."

I had never played a minute of hockey in my life. I hadn't watched it before Axel, hadn't known any of the rules.

But I knew something of aching to do what I loved.

I knew something of aching, of *wanting* something so bad, but that not mattering. Because my wants didn't factor into the universe's plan, didn't factor into my life. Of course, me wanting to be a teacher was nothing like the longing Stefan must be feeling watching some of his former teammates, watching his wife out there.

And not being able to help.

Especially in a game this big.

One of the Gold defensemen lost an edge and went sliding, losing their skate's grip on the ice, taking themselves out of the play, and in an instant, there was an odd man rush heading straight for Brit.

Stefan's wife didn't flounder, didn't hesitate, just challenged the players like the boss she was, making them force a pass across...

That Josh managed to get a stick on and deflect into the corner.

A second later, the game was rushing the other direction, and the Gold got a shot on net.

"So how do you handle it?" I asked once the goalie had frozen the puck and the game went to commercial break. "How do you handle being up here when they're down there?"

Stefan's smile was small. "You learn how to handle the agony." A beat. "And then you learn how to handle theirs when it doesn't work out."

TWELVE

AXEL

I'd never played in a game that had gone this far into double overtime.

The network was getting their money's worth, that was for damned sure.

But meanwhile, we were all dying on the ice, this slow war of attrition eating away at us piece by piece.

Exhaustion weighing down my legs.

Hands growing heavier by the moment.

This was the type of game where the series-deciding, the *Cup*-deciding goal wasn't going to be a pretty one, wasn't going to be a fluttering puck sailing across the ice and onto a teammate's stick who made a masterful deke and then chipped it into the top corner of the net.

Nope.

At this point in the game, it was going to bounce off someone's ass, squeak between the goalie's pads and the ice, barely cross that red goal line, or ricochet off a stick or skate or *several* sticks and skates.

Yup, it definitely was going to be an ugly ass goal.

And it was going to be heartbreaking for one of the teams.

But this game was going to end eventually.

Or at least, *that* was what I was telling myself.

Sweat was stinging my eyes. My feet were numb in my skates, which was an improvement on the cramping, aching pain from the previous ten minutes. My stick somehow had invisible weights attached to it, the negligible burden it had been for me to carry previously getting heavier by the shift. Hell, the puck had turned to iron, so much harder to move, sticking to the ice, requiring extra focus I didn't have available when I was mentally and physically exhausted.

"Yup. Yup!"

I glanced up, saw Josh breaking up the ice, somehow moving like he wasn't tired, like it didn't matter that we'd almost played two full games, one right after the other. Will was on with him, the two having created some excellent chemistry and chances in recent games, and this time was no exception. Will threaded the needle, sending the puck up to Josh's stick. Josh carried the puck into the zone, crossing over the blue line, closing in on the net and—

The crowd groaned.

I winced in solidarity.

Because fucking *ouch*.

Josh slammed into the ice, head bouncing off the hard surface, the puck squirting out from beneath him. The opposing team picked it up, started sprinting the other direction, and...

Fuck.

Josh wasn't moving.

But the officials wouldn't blow the whistle, not when the other team had possession of the puck and had a chance to score.

Not in game seven of the finals.

Not in double overtime of that game seven.

My fingers tightened on my stick as the players—four to our two—closed in on Brit.

I sucked in a breath and my lungs seized.

Fuck.

The puck slid from one side of the ice to the other.

Brit followed, keeping her angles, keeping her focus, trusting her defense to take the biggest threat while she tracked the puck, continued moving, never being caught flat-footed...

At least until her skate caught on something—a divot in the ice, a piece of tape, or maybe nothing, maybe she was just as tired as we were and she made a mistake.

Her feet slid out from beneath her.

She landed on the ice in an awkward heap, hard enough it must have stolen the air from her lungs, but even as the crowd gasped, as *I* gasped, she was recovering. Moving. Sliding.

But she was too slow and the other team was too close.

Half of the net was open.

Fuck.

My teeth clinked together, jaw aching from the force. My lungs weren't working and neither were my ears.

Time slowed down.

They were well over our blue line now.

The pass sailed back to the other side of the ice, splitting our defense.

Now they'd closed in on the top of the circles. One of their players dropped the puck back and—

"*Go.*"

Blood was dripping down Josh's face, and his eyes were wild, but he'd somehow made it to the bench.

"*Go!*" he said again.

I blinked.

Processed.

And then I was over the bench, skate blades hitting the ice, sprinting for our zone.

Coach hadn't told me to go—or maybe she had.

All I knew was that I was the closest and I'd reacted the fastest and suddenly I was on the ice. And heading for our zone.

But I didn't get there in time.

Brit was still on her side, scrambling to get her edges under her, to find her skates.

The four players for the other team had become five, and our forwards were hustling back to help our defense, but they still trail behind.

Five on two.

Brit made it to her knees.

The other team reached the hash marks.

A pass to the wide-open back door.

A pass that would allow the opposing player positioned there to just tap the puck home.

Fucking hell.

I couldn't get there in time.

None of us could.

All I could do was haul ass toward our zone, hope and pray to the hockey gods that I might make it in time to do *something*.

I wouldn't.

I *wouldn't* make it.

But luckily...I didn't need to.

The puck fluttered to that back door, landed on that players stick. He shot—

And Brit threw a leg encased in a broad, rectangular pad out.

It was that broad, rectangular pad that was our saving grace.

The puck hit the edge of that leather protective covering.

I sucked in a breath and everyone on the ice seemed to freeze, to hold their breath...

As the puck rolled just wide of the net.

It hit the boards with a soft *clink* that I swore I could hear, and maybe I did, maybe the entire arena had fallen silent, leaning forward on the edges of their seats, watching, waiting for that puck to go in the net.

And when it didn't...

The collective inhale was loud enough to hurt my ears.

Then Brit was on her feet.

Then Logan was at the boards, scooping up the puck, glancing up—

Electricity all along my spine.

I'd only gotten on the ice when Josh had made it to the boards.

I hadn't made much progress back-checking when Brit had somehow made that save.

Which meant I was behind all of their players.

Something that Logan saw.

Our eyes connected. That electricity fizzled. I started hauling ass.

Because I knew it was coming.

Logan fired the puck off the boards.

Turning as I scooped it up, feeling the sting of the impact with my stick blade in my palms. It was a good thing, jarring me to pinpoint focus. One that had me putting every bit of strength I still had left in me into my legs, into my hands.

Keep moving. Keep that puck on my stick blade.

Put distance between myself and their players.

Move. *Move.*

I *did* move.

Over the red line at center ice. Across their blue line.

Down over the tops of the circles.

To the hash marks at the midpoints of those circles, right into the slot that led to the front of the net.

I don't know how I knew what the goalie was going to do— maybe it was instinct, maybe it was knowledge buried somewhere in my mind from watching all that tape the video coaches had prepared for us.

Maybe it was just...luck.

But, regardless, I knew the goalie was going to try for a poke check.

He choked up on his stick. I swerved hard to the right, my skate blades digging into the ice with a sharp grinding sound.

I trusted them, trusted the equipment guys to have set me up for success, trusted my coaches to have drilled into me the knowledge and muscle memory I was using, trusted myself to know my limits.

The goalie's stick shot out.

The puck came with me...but only for a moment.

Because then I slid it beneath the outstretched stick and along the goalie's other side.

Toward the net.

THIRTEEN

BAILEY

He was skating so fast that he shot past the net, colliding with the boards, and landing in a heap that had me wincing.

That had to hurt.

But then I was looking away from him.

Because *where* was the puck?

Stefan was the first to process it, probably since he'd been down there many times before. He could just *see* better.

"It's in!" he shouted.

And I winced again—both from the shout and also because I jerked upright.

Because Stefan was right.

The puck *was* in the net.

Holy shit.

The puck was in the net.

A fact that everyone in the room, in the boxes, in the arena, on the ice, on those player benches down below at rink level seemed to realize all at once.

The. Puck. Was. *In*. The. Net.

I felt my mouth drop open as I glanced up at Stefan. He was smiling widely, gaze pointed on the screen.

I turned back to the TVs just in time to see the Gold sprint off the bench and mob Axel, taking him down to the ice under a dog pile of black and gold clad teammates. Smiles and fist-bumps and hugs and skates in the air and—

Axel emerging from the pile, his face stark, his eyes wide and surprised.

As though it hadn't hit him yet.

And then Brit moved up beside him—her helmet having joined the plethora of other equipment on the ice in a yard sale of epic proportions—and slung her arm around his shoulders, leaning close and saying something into his ear.

It was impossible to hear what she said, the crowd's cheers echoing even through the walls to where I was. It was impossible to read her lips, not with the chaos on the ice.

But whatever it was she said had that surprised look fading, had a smile spreading out on his face, a smile that was so fucking beautiful I immediately felt my eyes well with tears.

He must not have known or processed that he'd scored.

My beautiful, wounded, strong hockey player had scored the game-winning goal. During game seven. In double overtime. After the game had very nearly gone the absolute opposite way.

"They did it," I whispered.

Stefan gently touched my shoulder. "They did."

His eyes were glassy too, but I only caught a glimpse of those watery blue irises before he bent down and scooped up Roxie, hugging her tight. "Mama!" she shouted, pointing a chubby arm toward the TV.

"Yeah, baby," he said. "Mama did it." A glance up at me. "Everyone did it."

I bit my lip, nodding, and then turned back to the TV, watching the celebration, so fucking thrilled for them that I could barely take in the scene, could barely comprehend them shaking the other team's hands, barely saw the carpet being rolled out, the big silver cup being brought out to the ice.

The cheers grew louder, reverberating through the walls and humming in my belly, my heart.

My soul.

They'd done it.

And Axel was here for it.

Swear to Christ, my heart couldn't take it. This moment was too perfect, was too wonderful. But I didn't look away.

I just watched as Josh, a bandage around his head, red seeping through, moving stiffly, but upright, his smile huge, his hands reaching for the Cup. He lifted it from the podium, skated a small circle on the ice, and then...

Passed it to Axel.

Whose expression was one of shock, of awe, of reverence.

The crowd roared.

He skated...

And I felt it again in my veins, in my heart, in my soul.

His loop completed, I watched as he passed it to Brit, whose brown eyes were luminescent, her patented smile on full display.

Fucking beautiful.

Her. Him.

All of it.

"Want to take a walk down to ice level?" Stefan asked as Brit passed the Cup to Coop. "Or a hobble, rather?" he asked lightly, one half of his mouth turning up.

Right.

I had the big, dumb cast on, couldn't maneuver how I wanted, but I wasn't hurting right then. I wasn't feeling anything. I was running on happiness and adrenaline and whatever fucking pixie dust the fact that my boyfriend having just won the Stanley Cup created. I wasn't in pain. I—

Wanted to be in Axel's arms.

Was desperate to tell him how proud I was of him.

"Yeah," I told Stefan. "I'm ready for a hobble."

Grinning, he got my crutches for me, and I shoved them under my armpits, managed to get myself upright, to get my feet under me. I wanted to move quickly, but crutches were hard as fuck, and I was surviving on fumes, even if the adrenaline had temporarily banked my pain. Slow and steady was going to be my way forward.

It had helped me survive.

So I wouldn't discount it.

And that night it meant that I made slow, careful progress across the room. I made it into the elevator. I made it down to ice level.

I made it to the hallway that led to the ice.

Though, not on it, not like many of the families and kids and wives and girlfriends who were joining in on the celebration.

"Want me to help you?" Stefan had asked, Roxie on one hip, the little girl leaning so far forward it was a miracle he was able to hold her in place.

"No," I told him. "I don't think Axel would be happy if I took the crutches onto the ice."

And I wouldn't do anything to ruin this moment for him.

Plus, I'd survived a forest fire. I had a broken femur, burns and healing lungs and stitches. My mobility was limited to this slow hobbling around on crutches. I wasn't about to go out onto the ice and break my head and ass by trying to up my game and bring that slow hobbling onto a slippery surface.

I'd had enough pain for a good long while.

Stefan touched my cheek. "Probably not. I'll check in with you in a bit."

"Go," I ordered. "Be with your wife. Hug her tight for me for that save."

He grinned, and then he and Roxie were walking out onto the ice.

The fans noticed, the volume increasing as they caught sight of him, their love for the former captain still intense.

Brit moved to them and my ears rang as they embraced, my eyes stung.

It was the perfect end to her career—a hell of a game, winning it all, going out on top, and being able to skate right into her husband and daughter's arms, to have her daughter pulling her close and smacking a sloppy toddler kiss to her mouth.

Love. Family.

Perfect.

My eyes went beyond stinging.

They were leaking, dripping down my cheeks. Fuck, if six months ago I would have been able to predict that I would be here, feeling this way...I would have laughed myself silly.

I never *ever* could have imagined feeling this open, this in love, this *happy*.

Because the person *I* loved was here, had been part of all this amazingness.

Was—

A calloused thumb brushing the skin beneath my eyes. "Who do I have to kill for these tears?" Axel asked softly, towering over me in his skates, his skin flushed, his hair sweaty and mussed from his helmet.

And still, he was the most beautiful man I'd ever seen.

I smiled up at him. "The man who scored the game-winning goal."

His cheeks went a little more pink. "It was nothing."

I leaned into him, reaching up, the crutches slipping free and falling to the black skate mats. But he had me, it was never a thought that he wouldn't. Reaching up, way up, I cupped his cheeks. "I am so *freaking* proud of you."

A shake of his head. "I—"

"You," I whispered. "I am so proud of *you*, honey."

His arms banded tightly around me and he buried his face in my hair.

Then his shoulders began to shake.

And I knew my big, broody hockey player had lost it.

Fourteen

Axel

My heart was pumping.

The crowd was cheering.

The ice was full of people.

But the woman I loved was in my arms, and she had helped me accomplish something amazing.

So, yeah, admittedly, I lost it for a moment.

These last couple of days had been a lot, and having Bailey in my arms, hearing her say she was proud of me...

Hell, it fucked with my tough hockey player image, but I couldn't deny that my eyes were full of tears—and that maybe a few of them escaped. And truthfully, I couldn't give a fuck if the cameras caught that.

Because Bailey was my heart.

Her hands went to my hair, holding me to her.

And I just sat in this moment, soaked in the way it felt when she held me, breathed through the fact that I'd just been part of a team to win a Cup, that we'd won because of a goal *I'd* scored.

It was the stuff of lying in bed as a kid, lying on a bare mattress, my one blanket tucked over me, staring at the stained ceiling overhead and fantasizing to drown out my reality—to drown out my mom, who was fucking some guy in the other room or drunk and pounding on my door, pissed because I hadn't done something (on the odd times she remembered I was there at all) or yelling at whoever she was fucking because she was drunk or because she was pissed that he hadn't brought her enough booze.

I'd dreamed then.

Wished then.

But never really accepted that it could actually happened.

And today it had.

"Fuck, buttercup," I whispered.

Her fingers dug into my jersey, into my shoulder pads where the bottom part wrapped around the back of my ribcage.

I felt the slight bite of her nails, knew she felt just as flayed open as I did. "Yes," she whispered. "*That.*"

I chuckled and leaned back enough to see her face. "You hurting?"

"In the best way," she whispered, rubbing the space on her chest, beneath which sat that beautiful heart.

Fuck, she was so fucking sweet. Bending, I slanted my mouth over hers, dipping my tongue into her mouth and kissing her way too deep and way too long considering there were people and cameras all around.

And case in point—

The cheers grew loud enough that I lifted my head, saw that we were on the jumbotron.

Her cheeks were pink, but she just glanced at the camera and waved...to more cheers.

"You're amazing," I said when she looked back to me.

Her inhale was shaky. "I love you." Our eyes locked and time stretched between us—just us, just our love and our lives and being thankful we were right here in this moment. But eventually, we managed to tear our gazes apart, to look back out at the ice. "You should go back out there," she murmured, leaning her head against my arm.

"Come with me."

"I know I'm stubborn and like to do everything on my own," she said, turning her head and pressing a kiss to my biceps—or at least where my biceps would be if my jersey and my shoulder and elbow pads hadn't been in the way. "But even I don't think I can manage the ice on my crutches."

"Who says you need your crutches?" I asked lightly.

The little vee that appeared between her brows made me want to kiss her all over again. "Um, the *doctor* says I need my crutches, and for that matter so do yo—*ah!*"

I swept her up, careful to support her leg, making sure to not bump it on anyone or on any of the equipment or on boards or... well, just making sure to not ram her broken leg into something. Luckily, when I got out onto the ice there was more room, even though it was crawling with family members and back-office staff and players and—

I carefully set her down, waiting until she was steady on her good foot, still taking a good portion of her weight so that I could make sure that she was safe, wasn't going to slip and fall.

"Axel," she breathed, almost too soft for me to hear over the din.

"I know, buttercup," I whispered.

And then we just stood there at center ice, staring up at the stands, at the crowd, watching my teammates take their turn with the Cup, and I knew she felt much of what I felt, knew she was as awed as I was.

It was in her eyes, her expression, in the way that she leaned up and kissed my jaw.

A miracle.

A dream.

A future I was never going to let go.

Because she was in my arms.

It was just after dawn and I hadn't slept a wink.

We'd stayed at the rink too long, had spent way too much time with the guys in the locker room, had done too many fucking interviews.

But eventually, I'd managed to get away, to convince Bailey that we'd stayed long enough.

The team would be getting together later today. The party would continue.

My woman had needed her bed.

She hadn't said a word about being tired or wanting to go—of course she hadn't, of course she *wouldn't*. But I'd watched her lids droop and the fatigue write itself into the lines of her face.

Stubborn, though.

She'd refused to leave several times over and because the celebration and press and staff were all around, everyone wanting to be part of this moment, we'd stayed.

Until I'd looked over and seen her propped in the corner of the locker room, back against the wall, leg propped up on the bench, Roxie curled up in her lap. They were both fast asleep, and though I'd paused to take a picture, because—fuck—who wouldn't want to document all of that beauty, after I'd managed to signal to Stefan.

We'd tag-teamed our women to the car—minus Brit, who'd stayed behind to finish speaking to all of the media and the few lucky fans who'd been allowed behind the scenes.

Bailey had protested when I'd carried her through the halls, but she was exhausted and plus, Stefan, had found her crutches and was carrying both them and Roxie, so Bailey hadn't been able to stubborn herself outside on them.

She'd fallen asleep in the car.

I'd gotten her up to the apartment, tucked into bed, thankful that Stefan had given me the bottle of pain medicine before he'd left with Roxie, because I'd managed to rouse her enough to take them. Then I'd gone back to the car, retrieved her crutches and settled into bed beside her.

Pitch black night had given way to the early morning, navy creeping into reds and oranges and yellows as the sun began to rise in the east.

And still I didn't sleep.

Not because I wasn't tired.

I was exhausted, so tired it was pulling at my bones, sinking my body heavy into the mattress, tendrils winding their hooks into the edges of my mind, drawing me down.

But I couldn't sleep.

Not a surprise.

I was replaying the game. And then I was going over the last few days. And then I was thinking about how everything could have easily turned out so, so differently, and just wanting to close my eyes, to let sleep drag me under.

But it was like I was waiting for something.

Or maybe part of me was worried that the moment I *did* fall asleep, I'd wake up and realize this had all been a dream.

I'd wake up and I'd be right back in that nightmare.

I'd wake up and—

My phone rang.

That wasn't unusual. It had been going off for hours, pinging with texts, buzzing with calls, voicemails stacking up.

But when I glanced at the screen, my spine froze solid.

Because I knew that even though I had stayed awake...

The nightmare was going to yank me under anyway.

Fifteen

For a minute, I didn't know where I was.

The ranch. The hospital bed. No...

In Axel's apartment. In his bedroom. In his arms.

I started to roll toward him, but he dropped his hand onto my hip, holding me steady. "Easy, buttercup," he murmured, stopping me from rolling over onto my broken leg.

Smart man, he was.

He shifted, coming over me, his hand braced by my head, his eyes coming to mine.

God, he was pretty.

And mine.

"Hi, honey," I murmured, reaching up, stroking my fingers through the thick brown beard coating his jaw.

"Hi," he murmured back.

"Stanley Cup Champion," I whispered, my lips turning up into a grin I could feel was taking over my whole face.

His eyes were full of emotion. "Because of you."

I shook my head.

"I never would have made it this far," he said softly. "Not without you."

"Dammit!" I hissed, feeling the burn in the corners of my eyes. This *man*.

"What?" he asked, lips tipping up again before he bent and brushed them over my forehead. "Because I'm going to make you cry?"

"Yes." A huff. "I'm not a crier. I'm a tough cowgirl who kicks ass on my ranch, but you—" Except, my words caught up with me and now my eyes stung for a whole other reason.

My ranch was gone.

I knew it.

I *felt* it.

The fire had moved too quickly, had burned too fast, swooping down the hills toward the barn, toward the house.

God, Gramps and Gran's place.

My place.

The pictures, the horseshoe over the door, the wine barrel pots filled with cheerful flowers.

Gone.

"Hey," he said softly, covering my hand with his own, lacing our fingers together. "It's okay."

It wasn't.

Not really.

The incandescent joy of the night before had been punctured by reality, had been burned to ashes by the hot licking flames that left blisters on my arms and my lungs weak and my hair singed.

"It's gone," I whispered.

His face gave me the answer I already knew, but *fuck* it still hurt so freaking much.

"Tommy, Hank, and Eli?" I asked, mind racing away from that pain. "Are their places—?" But I didn't finish the question, because the look that entered his eyes when I said their names sent a dagger directly into my heart.

"No," I whispered, tears escaping in earnest now. "*No.*"

I had to be reading Axel wrong.

Maybe their *ranches* were gone, but it couldn't be what I was seeing in Axel's eyes, couldn't be the truth that was roaring through me about those flames that had moved so quickly, burned so hotly.

"*No*," I said again when Axel's face didn't clear, when that heavy, *sad* look didn't leave his eyes. "*No!*"

"Honey," he whispered.

And that was enough. It sliced through me, had the truth settling on me with all the force of an atom bomb.

The tears didn't just burn my eyes, didn't just singe my cheeks, they hitched through my body in wracking, painful sobs, rending my heart, my bones, my *soul*. Axel shifted to my side, tugged my body against his, arms holding me tight. I felt him distantly, because I couldn't be there, couldn't be truly present in my body, not in that moment.

I was thinking of Tommy and Hank and Eli, thinking about how they'd taken me under their wings, how they'd helped me fight to keep Gramps' ranch going. I was thinking of the pride in their eyes when they'd agreed to my plan for extra income. I was thinking of them showing up with hay and fixing my tractor and answering all of the questions that had been generated from a young, naive girl taking over a failing ranch.

And now they were gone.

"How?" I eventually managed to whisper.

A long pause. Then Axel smoothed his knuckles over my cheek, said softly, "Frank said the fire just moved too fast. They couldn't get out, even with your warning."

Fuck.

Fuck.

Another sob wracking my body, and then he was holding me again. Not telling me to stop. Not telling me it would be okay. Just wrapping me in his arms and pressing me close, my ear to his chest, his heartbeat steady beneath his rib cage.

That pulsing, even rhythm eventually settled me.

"I'm sorry," he said long minutes later, his fingers sliding through my hair.

"I know," I whispered. "But *I'm* the one who's sorry. I ruined your post-Cup—"

His fingers tightened slightly and he tilted my head up, eyes locking onto mine. "Don't you dare apologize."

"But I—"

"Don't," he repeated, tucking my head back into his throat, his fingers going to my hair again, drifting through the ends. "Just don't, buttercup."

So, I didn't.

I didn't make further apologies and I didn't harp on the fact that I was crying on the morning after he'd achieved something huge, bringing the mood down, even if it was an accident and things were raw and I hadn't meant to turn into a sobbing woman in his arms.

Because everything was so fucking heavy and I needed someone to help me shoulder the burden, at least for a little bit.

I was homeless. I'd lost everything. People I loved were gone. My home and town were destroyed. My body was broken.

So, I just stayed in those arms.

Just let him hold me.

Just listened to his heartbeat in my ear.

It was steady, so steady, and that steady was the single thing grounding me to this world.

For now, that was enough.

———

He'd driven through the smoke-filled roads, drawing us closer to River's Bend.

But that wasn't our destination.

Not at first, anyway.

The fire was fifty percent contained, though the firefighters had managed to keep it from engulfing any more towns as they encircled the blaze. It would probably be weeks before it was fully out, before the smoke fully cleared, but they'd begun allowing people back into town to see what remained.

Many of River's Bend's residents were still in the shelter, still staying at hotels and motels along the highway, miles from town, miles from whatever remained of their homes.

I needed to see them.

Needed to see Dessie and Ryan, Billie Rose and Joel. Needed to see my friends. Needed to make sure they were okay.

Axel had said the only casualties were on the ranches on my side of town.

But I *needed* to see the people I loved.

So, I'd crammed myself into his car, endured the uncomfortable drive, and convinced Axel to first take me to the shelter and then up to River's Bend.

Now, as the smoke got thicker along both sides of the road, clawing its way between the trees, my nerves were prickling uncomfortably.

My throat was tight.

My skin stung in memory.

My fingers formed tight, tight fists.

"We can go back," Axel murmured, reaching over and carefully loosening my hold, lacing our fingers together. "Do this another day."

Was the smell of smoke triggering me?

Were my lungs already feeling tight?

Yup. And yup.

But I needed to do this, to see them, see my friends, needed to know that th-they'd survived and were okay when the others weren't.

I tightened my grip on his hand. "No," I whispered. "I need to do this."

A nod. No further arguments.

Just holding my hand, taking us through the smoke-filled road, and turning into a parking lot.

It was for a neighboring town's high school, I realized, my eyes just able to make out the concrete sign, the letters etched into the surface.

He parked in the ash-covered lot, pressed a kiss to the back of my hand.

Then he released me and was out through his door, rounding the hood, and opening mine. "Ready?"

A soft question.

My big broody hockey player all soft and gentle, but only for me.

I nodded, let him pull me up and out of my seat, holding on to the top of the car until he retrieved my crutches from the back seat.

Under my armpits.

Hobbling my way inside...

What I didn't realize was that I would be hobbling my way into hell.

Sixteen

Axel

I felt the shock go through Bailey and moved a little closer to her, wishing that I could hold her hand, that I could hold *her*. Because I knew exactly what she was feeling.

This was hell on earth.

Dogs barking in wire crates, blankets tossed over the top in a valiant hope that they might quiet, might find some peace amid all this chaos. Kids sat on cots, their eyes wide and shocked, all of them too quiet, staring off into space like they were living their own personal nightmare.

And they were.

Their town as they knew it was gone.

So they were in a nightmare. Living it, surrounded by it.

I thought of the phone call I'd received in the early hours of that morning while Bailey slept in my arms.

Knew that I understood something of living in a personal nightmare.

How life could swivel from one extreme to the other in just a few days was unfathomable, *untenable*.

But this wasn't about me, not right now.

This was about Bailey and Billie Rose, who I could see organizing supplies in the far corner of the room. This was about Joel beside her, shifting boxes. This was about Dessie, laying out food on the folding tables set up along one side of the gym.

This was about the people of River's Bend.

This was about finding ways to help them.

"Billie is over there," I said, leaning in to whisper in Bailey's ear and pointing toward her aunt. "Can you make it over there, buttercup? Or do you want me to go get her?"

A shuddering breath. "I can make it."

No surprise there, I thought, smothering a smile.

This wasn't the place for smiles, even though I was beyond glad to see a glimpse of my woman in amongst all this awfulness.

We picked our way over to Billie Rose, pausing when Bailey needed to give her ribs, her body a break.

A few people spoke to her, to me, checking in on her injuries, offering quiet congratulations for the game, but I felt very far removed from the victory of the night before. There were no winners here—everyone in this gymnasium had lost something or someone.

"You need to take a break."

Not me ordering Bailey to rest, though it sounded very much like something that would come out of my mouth.

Instead, it was from Joel, who looked like he'd been pulled backward through a hedge.

"I'm fine."

That was a statement that sounded like it could have come from Bailey, demonstrating all that stubborn.

But then again Bailey and Billie Rose *were* related, so it wasn't a surprise that stubborn ran in their DNA.

It also wasn't a surprise that Joel was giving orders.

My former teammate and I had similarities aside from hockey —being annoying and bossy with a tinge of asshole, at least according to Bailey. Joel was nicer than me, though. Although not with Billie Rose. With Bailey's aunt...well, buttons were pushed.

Regularly.

And she returned the favor.

Oil and water. Enemies united solely for a common cause but prepared to stab each other in the back at the first opportunity.

Hell, I'd heard Joel refer to Billie Rose as *harpy* more than a few times.

But there was no *harpy* in sight, not on his tongue, not in his eyes. Just concern and orders to rest and—

Bailey glanced up at me, lifted her brows, the first lick of mischief I'd seen on her face since finding her in that forest making my breath catch.

God, she was gorgeous.

God, she was *mine*.

Joel snagged Billie's arm. "I said you need—"

A jerk, Billie Rose stepping back. "And *I* said I'm *fine*. I need to sort these supplies and get them over to the other shelter." She yanked a box out of the stack and did it so abruptly that she nearly toppled backward. *Would* have toppled backward if not for Joel catching her.

Bailey looked up at me again, her brows still raised, that mischief glowing bright, and this time, I couldn't smother my smile.

Because I was thinking the same thing that my woman clearly was.

Sparks. Irritation. Bickering. Trying very hard to stay away from each other.

And it had ended up with us in love, with me absolutely devoted to this woman who held my heart, knowing we had ties between us that would never be broken.

"You're about to collapse," Joel snapped, so focused on Billie that he hadn't noticed our approach. Or maybe he had and he didn't care, his worry and attention solely for the blond firecracker who took planning and preparation and love for her town to a critical level. "The black circles beneath your eyes have their own fucking black circles. You need to lay down for an hour and then can get back to it. You won't do anyone any good if you burn out, sweetheart."

Billie finally released the box, setting it down with a *thump*. "I'm not your *sweetheart*," she snapped, jabbing a finger into his chest.

Joel snagged her wrist. "Okay, *sweetheart*, so I'll go back to harpy."

She tugged, nostrils flaring, gritting out, "Let me go."

Joel didn't.

I could practically see the smoke coming out of her ears, but curiosity had gripped me and I found that I couldn't bring myself to interrupt. Not when I wanted to see how this played out.

"Ugh!" she growled, pairing the animalistic sound with a stomp of her foot, looking ready to close the nearly two feet of distance between herself and Joel and clock him over the head... probably with that box.

It was heavy, but she was motivated.

And *I* was thoroughly entertained.

Bailey, apparently, thought it was prudent to intervene. "Billie," she murmured.

Her aunt jumped about three feet in the air.

I smoothed a hand down Bailey's back, stopping probably too close to that lush ass of hers, considering we were in public. "I was enjoying the show, buttercup," I murmured in her ear.

An arch look in my direction. "Behave."

"You first," I grumbled and nipped the dangling lobe.

Another arch look, but relief slid through me when she leaned back against my body, letting me have some of her weight. I knew from experience that crutches were a pain to use, not to mention, seriously hard work, especially given the span of her injuries.

"See?" she muttered. "Behaving. Now you."

"Never," I teased, pressing my lips to the spot behind her ear, the one that always made her shiver. "And you don't want me to."

She rewarded my insolence with a kiss to my jaw, made easier because I'd bent down to her ear, hadn't been able to resist being as close as possible to her, even with the difference in our heights. "That's true, honey," she murmured and she gave me more of her weight. I soaked in this bit of light, this bit of humor on her face because I knew, *knew* that it was going to get tougher from here. Knew that the light would be blocked out by the dark clouds of reality soon enough.

Another kiss to my jaw, then she returned her attention back to her aunt, just as Billie Rose and Joel managed to stop focusing on each other and spun to face us.

To Joel's credit, Billie *did* look exhausted—lines around her mouth, her eyes, those dark circles certainly prominent. Her face was pale and streaked with ash, same as her hair.

She needed a shower and a bed for a good ten hours.

But Billie Rose was a force, and I wasn't going to be the one who could force her there.

Bailey might succeed.

Or Joel, I thought, biting back the smirk.

Billie moved toward us, gently cupping Bailey's cheeks. "You look good, honey," she said, moving in and carefully hugging her niece (yes, they were almost the same age; yes, that was weird; also yes, thinking about Bailey being Billie's niece was weird, even though it was true). "I'm glad to see you up and around. I thought after last night you'd be sleeping the day away."

"Axel's been making me rest and take my medicine. Funny how that works and makes me feel better," Bailey said dryly.

Billie Rose's piercing blue eyes hit mine, approval and gratitude in those depths.

I didn't need the latter—Bailey was my heart and I'd give everything of mine to take care of her. The former, I couldn't lie, the former felt good.

I hadn't had a lot of approval in my life.

My fault, yes.

But also not something I'd grown up with.

Which was a line of thinking I didn't want to go down, not after that morning, and—

No.

I sliced straight through that thought, cutting it off in its tracks.

Later, I'd worry about phone calls and the bullshit I grew up with and all the things that made up my nightmares.

Right now, we needed to deal with the problem at hand.

SEVENTEEN

"You get your aunt to rest," Axel murmured in my ear, his hot breath making me shiver. "I'll take Joel."

My brows dragged together, not sure why he'd need to take Joel.

But then I took a closer look at the man who'd stepped in, protecting me from my abusive, asshole ex when he didn't have to put his neck on the line, not for me, a relative stranger. That closer look showed me enough.

Because the big, broody hockey player who was hovering by my aunt was equally as exhausted.

He was complaining about her dark circles?

Well, his were big, broody hockey player sized. And paired with enough lines of fatigue drawn into his face to form a roadmap, stubble that was long and scraggly, even for a big, broody hockey player, and I understood precisely why Axel was going to take him.

Glancing up at *my* big, broody hockey player, I nodded in

agreement then crutched forward to Billie. "Show me around," I demanded. "I need to do something to help."

"You should rest—"

I lifted my brows. "Is this where I say I'm rubber and you're glue?"

A frown, her blond curls bouncing.

I just held her eyes, waited.

Until she huffed, those curls bouncing again, and then she spun on her heel. "Fine. You can help over here."

Since over *here* was closer to several empty cots, these in a more isolated corner of the gym, I nodded and followed her.

When I'd made it to her, she was dragging several boxes over so they were within arm's reach of those cots. I glanced back, saw Joel start to me toward us, his expression thunderous, but Axel stepped in front of him, and I watched, waiting to see what would happen.

Terse words.

That thunderous look darkening.

But eventually, Joel spun on his heel and stormed away.

Letting out a silent breath, I turned my attention back to Billie Rose and wondered if I would need to tackle my aunt to get her to chill the fuck out for an hour or two to get her to stop sorting through boxes that didn't need sorting, just because she had to find something to keep her busy.

So she didn't think.

So she wouldn't be sucked down into the sad.

Because I knew my aunt.

She would be the rock, the tough one, the person who everyone turned to, and she wouldn't allow herself to be sad, to feel, to sit and cry and grieve for what they'd lost.

She'd hide behind that wall of capability.

Until people stopped trying to help her.

But today, I was there.

Today, I was *going* to help her.

No arguments.

Now I just needed to figure out how to get her to lie down for a few minutes without tackling her to the cot, because I was damn sure if I *did* tackle her in an effort to get her to rest, that she wouldn't hesitate to launch me off her and onto the floor in order to keep on with her busying.

And that launching would hurt.

And I'd had enough things hurting for a while.

For a *damned* long while.

"We need to sort these," Billie said. "To split them up into smaller sets." She dropped another box onto the one she'd set in front of the cot. "Pair them together with"—turning, she scooped up a third box—"these and put them all"—another box landed uncomfortably close to my toes...the ones on the broken leg—"in here." She clapped her hands together, started to turn away. "Good? *Good.*"

She began to walk back toward the original stack of boxes.

"Um, Billie?"

My aunt froze, her shoulders hitching up so tightly that they were practically at her ears. "Yeah?"

"Can you help me sit down so I can do this?" I asked, nodding at my leg and the crutches when she spun to face me. "I can't—" I tilted my head toward the cot. "I can't sit all that easily."

A pause.

Her impatience almost palpable.

But Billie Rose was also a caretaker, and I knew that she couldn't—and thus *wouldn't*—leave me to struggle down to sitting by myself.

She made me wait a good long time for her help, though.

Eyes narrowed, lips pressed flat, jaw clenched.

A sigh.

Then she was back at my side, wrapping her fingers around an uninjured part of my arm, easing the crutches away and helping me onto my ass.

Ouch.

I hissed out a breath.

"Shoot," she said loosening her grip. "Are you okay? Did I hurt you?"

It *all* hurt, including Billie's hold on her arm, but it wasn't anything my aunt was doing. It was just...because I'd been trapped in a wildfire and was dealing with burns and stitches and a broken leg and bruised ribs. *Everything* hurt.

"I'm fine," I said. "Just..." I released a breath, the pain subsiding. "Sit here and let me lean against you."

"You should be in bed." But Billie dutifully sank down next to me.

"I've spent all my energy fighting with Axel about going to the game, about coming here today." I dropped my head on her shoulder, sighed. "I don't have any energy left to fight with you."

"Yeah, tell me about wasting energy fighting," Billie Rose muttered.

I smothered my smile. "Joel's superpower does seem to be pissing you off."

A snort.

"You know, *I* know something about fighting with a big, broody hockey player."

Billie tugged my hair.

"Ow!" I rubbed a hand to my stinging scalp. *That* had been the one part of me that hadn't hurt.

"Behave," she grumbled, tucking me back against her. "Joel is an ass."

"A good-looking ass who can't keep his eyes off you," I pointed out.

She threatened to pull my hair again. "Hilarious."

"I'm not joking."

A sigh. "I'm not having this conversation with you."

There was a finality to her tone that had me backing off. But because I was me and she was my aunt and one of my closest friends, I let it go (with just one more comment). "Also, just saying, hockey players have the best asses."

She turned to glare at me, but my comment had her shaking a head, lips turning up at the edges. "You think you're hilarious."

"I think that I'm glad you're okay."

Her throat bobbed, eyes going glassy. "Me too, honey." A beat. "God, Bay, you scared the crap out of me."

"*I* scared the crap out of *me*."

"When we found your trailer on the road…"

Fear in my belly, in my throat, remembering the flames closing in, the road blocked ahead, the desperate scramble to get Picard and Data out of the trailer.

I inhaled. "I know," I whispered. "It was…I was really scared, Bil."

My aunt slipped an arm around me, held me close. "I know, honey. I'm sorry that happened."

"Tom, Hank, and Eli—" My voice broke, cutting off my words.

"You heard," she whispered.

"I—" My throat was tight. "I heard."

"I'm sorry."

"*I'm* sorry," I said. "If I'd seen the fire sooner, had gotten the warning out before—"

I gasped when Billie spun to face me, hand coming to my jaw, glare fixing me in place. "You have nothing to apologize for. *Nothing*." She shook my face lightly. "Your call is why the only deaths were because the fire moved so fast by the ranches. *You're* the reason we were able to use the evacuation plan, why we were able to get everyone out."

I started to shake my head. I'd made a call. That was it.

Billie and the rest of them had gotten everyone safe.

"Look around you, Bay." Billie swung out an arm. "This is because of you."

I inhaled, knowing I could keep arguing, but that wasn't

getting Billie to rest. That was keeping her up, triggering her dog-to-a-bone mentality.

So I covered her hand with my own, agreed, "Yes." Though, not able to completely let it go, I added, "But it's also because of us."

Eighteen

Axel

I glanced over, watching Bailey sitting with Billie Rose, the pair lost in a serious conversation.

I didn't think it was about Joel being an annoying bastard.

But I wouldn't put it past them either.

"She needs to rest," Joel—speak of the devil (or annoying bastard)—muttered. "She's been up for two straight days."

"You'd only know that," I pointed out, "if you'd been up with her for those two days."

A shrug. "I'm used to going without sleep. You know we are."

Late nights. Aborted sleep. Schedules that were fucked six ways to Sunday. Yeah, Joel and I knew plenty about surviving on minimal rest, and that wasn't even during a fucking emergency.

But we could only maintain that for so long.

"She'll be more likely to rest when if you do it yourself. You know it's true," I added when he opened his mouth to protest.

"No," he muttered, "she'll probably take the opportunity to stay up for another twelve hours."

"Bailey's got her."

I nodded toward the two of them sitting on the cot, still talking, though Billie's eyelids were looking droopier by the second.

Give my woman a few more minutes and the mayor of River's Bend was going to be sprawled out on that cot, dead asleep.

"Right," Joel muttered. "So help me move these boxes."

I didn't argue. Joel was a stubborn asshole, and I wouldn't get through his thick, dumb head with a straight on attack.

So, I helped with the boxes.

I stacked them where he directed—which was actually in several different spots—and opened the ones he ordered me to open. Then I was distributing the supplies inside to the correct locations—food to the kitchen and tables set out for people to grab what they needed, clothes hung up on the proper racks, organized by size, underwear and socks similarly sorted and in boxes down below, water and other drinks in coolers, first aid supplies to the nurses' station with simpler things like bandages and antibiotic cream in small baskets just outside the door.

Trying to be thoughtful about balancing the people who were staying here having access to what they needed and making certain that all of the proper materials were with the people who needed them to help whoever might seek them out.

Once we'd finished with the boxes, I managed to shove a plate of food into Joel's hand—thanks to Dessie and her being aware of him burning the candle at both ends.

We moved over to the bleachers, half-unfolded to leave lots of space open for the cots, and climbed to the top, taking a bird's eye view of the space and leaning against the wall, pieces of the huge mural of the mountain lion—this school's mascot—visible above the worn wood.

It had been a long time since I'd been in a school gymnasium, but it felt similar to those high school years.

The buzz of conversation.

The squeak of shoes on the hardwood.

The emotions that were filling up the space.

Of course, there wasn't any excitement, just disappointment and frustration and sadness, like their team had lost the biggest game of the year.

Not a surprise given the circumstances.

I'd taken a plate too, even though Bailey and I had eaten on the way up. Not because I was hungry, but because I didn't think Joel would stop and sit down with me unless I was stuffing my face too.

And, hell, I was happy to be off the team diet plan for a few months.

Costco muffins the size of my head sounded like a damned good plan.

I peeled the wrapper of the chocolate muffin with chocolate chips, was about to take a huge bite when Joel's head suddenly shot up and he seemed to actually see *me* for the first time since I'd come in. "Fuck, man," he said, his plate forgotten on his lap. "You won the Cup."

My lips twitched. "Yeah, we did."

We, not *I* because I couldn't have done it without it the rest of my team. Because, while my contribution might have come at the right moment, I definitely couldn't say that it was any more important than the save Brit had made a half-minute before, than the hit Logan had laid out in game three, than the consistency Blue and Coop and Will and Rome had brought throughout the entire season.

Now that I'd gotten my head out of my ass, I'd finally figured out what a team could be like.

Something I could have had years before if not for said head in ass.

"How's it feel?"

I sighed, setting my muffin onto my plate, not doing Joel the disservice of giving him a canned answer. This was my former teammate. This was a man who'd had my back more times than I could ever count, who'd had Bailey's back.

He deserved consideration and a thoughtful answer.

And, truthfully, I hadn't really thought about how it felt.

Other than *good*.

Ha.

That was real deep and reflective, and maybe six months ago, the notion of me being deep and reflective would have been the most hilarious joke I'd ever heard. Today, it wasn't. Today, I was different. I'd grown.

Look at me go!

Snorting inwardly, I met Joel's green eyes, saw that some of the tension that had been present in them from the moment Bailey and I had walked into the gym had faded. Or, well, since Bailey had crutched and I'd walked in behind her, enjoying the view of her ass that I fucking dreamed about (or, rather, dreamed about fucking) in the leggings that were tight enough to caress her curves.

They'd been a bitch to get over her cast, but the view I'd enjoyed while trailing her had made that struggle well worth it.

I was a sick bastard.

Luckily, my woman loved it.

Joel shifted next to me, and right, I was supposed to be answering him, not playing inner monologue.

"It feels..." I shoved a chunk of the muffin in my mouth, chewed as I pondered that question. "I guess it still feels surreal and strange and not *real*, you know?" I said once I'd swallowed.

Joel nodded, gaze drifting out onto the floor, toward a certain pair of women, sitting on a certain set of cots, though the one with blond curls was currently sprawled on one of the fold-out beds. "You had quite a span of experiences this year," he murmured, seemingly tearing his eyes away, bringing them back to mine, though, I couldn't help but note them sliding back to the cots just a few heartbeats later.

But, focus on Billie Rose or not, Joel spoke the truth.

I'd had quite a run of it over the last months.

Almost washing out of the AHL and making a name for

myself as solely a troublemaker, to NHL roster spot fill-in, to getting a permanent contract on a team that was a contender for the playoffs, to winning the Cup by putting in the game-winning goal.

Big things.

Once-in-a-lifetime *huge* things.

But not one of those things was as important as Bailey.

Not even the family I'd become part of with the Gold.

And yeah, did that make me a sappy fuck? Both because I was all in on the family talk and because I was thinking my buttercup was the heart of my heart, that my soul sang for just one her, for that wonderful fucking woman and no one else on this planet? Yes. I was sappy. I was in love. I wasn't scared to think about it.

Not any longer.

I saw it for the gift it was.

"Maybe it'll sink in at some point," I told Joel. "But right now —especially with all of this"—I waved my hand at the gym, at the people, the cots, at the fact that we were in this shelter in the first place—"it hasn't quite settled that deep."

"I feel that."

I shoved another bite into my mouth, chewed and swallowed. "I almost lost her," I whispered into the silence that had fallen between us. "And I would have lost everything. None of it would have meant *anything*. The win. The goal. The Cup. It would have all been just...*nothing*."

Silence.

But then he dropped his hand onto my knee, squeezed tightly. "She's your person."

"Yeah," I agreed.

The quiet fell again.

Then I couldn't resist saying, "And I'm starting to think that Billie Rose is—"

"Don't," he snapped.

"She's smart, driven, and local," I pointed out.

"*Don't*," he repeated.

"And you're protective over her, and she pushes your buttons. Plus, she has a great ass and—"

He shoved me. "Cut it out, fuckhead."

"—and," I repeated, ignoring him, "there are sparks for days, man." A beat. "So much so that you can't keep your eyes off her, even when she's sleeping."

Joel tore said eyes away from the cots in the corner of the room, glaring at me.

I grinned, shoved the rest of my muffin into my mouth.

"Just saying."

Did it sound like *jush shayling?* Yes.

Did I give a fuck?

No.

Especially, if it meant that it would help Joel find his person.

NINETEEN

BAILEY

We'd left Joel sleeping on the cot next to Billie Rose, blankets tucked up around both of their chins, boxes sorted, the shelter as stocked and organized as possible. For the moment anyway.

The winds were dying down, and the smoke was beginning to clear—or at least, not being pushed toward River's Bend.

So more people would be leaving the shelters.

Some going home—a precious few whose homes were safe and utilities would soon be restored to. Some moving onto hotels or apartments or friends or family—places they could stay until they were able to rebuild. Some would be staying in the shelter for a bit longer, having no place to move on to. And some...some would be leaving and never returning to town.

The fear too great.

The devastation too close to home.

That hurt my heart in the worst way.

But I was tabling that hurt for the moment. There would be time to wrap it around me later, to let it bring out my tears. Deep in the night, when the world was quiet and my mind didn't want to settle.

Now, I was struggling to keep my breathing even, my pulse steady.

Because fear was sitting heavy in my belly, clawing deeply and dragging it talons through my soul.

Heat and smoke.

Terror and knowing I was going to die.

Losing—

Axel's fingers lacing with mine, holding tight, steadying me without a word.

The talons loosened and I glanced up at him, saw that he'd stopped on the bridge outside of town, not driving across it.

Waiting.

Until I was ready.

Fuck, I loved this man.

Looking away from his eyes that saw right through my shield, my mask I was trying to keep in place. If I could just pretend that I would be okay, then I would *be* okay.

But that hadn't ever been true.

That was what had landed me in a relationship that had nearly destroyed me.

Hiding from the truth, brutal and fearful and painful. Pretending, masking what was really inside my heart.

I wasn't that woman anymore.

Because of the man next to me. Because of *me.*

So, I owed both of us the truth.

Fuck the masks.

Let me be *me.*

I held his fingers tighter, swallowed hard against the knot in my throat and whispered, "I'm scared."

His fingers grasped mine, holding just as tight, keeping me grounded into this moment and not the past. "I'm scared, too."

Whoa.

That surprised me.

Because...well, I don't know why it surprised me.

He'd been here, searching for me, surely panicked. God knew, *I* would have been freaking the fuck out if a fire had burned through his town while I'd been away, not able to contact him, just watching the news grow more and more grim with every special report.

"So we do it together?" I asked, lifting our interlaced hands and pressing them to my chest, to the spot over where my heart pounded hard against my ribcage.

"Do we do things any other way?"

That had my lips twitching. "No," I said. "Not anymore anyway."

Fingers brushing my hair off my forehead. "That's the correct answer."

"Well," I mock-grumbled. "You don't have to be all cocky about it."

A lifted brow. A smirk that I loved. "Yeah, buttercup. I *do* have to be all *cocky* about it."

I snorted. "That was bad, even for you."

Laughter, beautiful, *Axel* laughter rang through the car.

That was my man. That was the man I loved.

"Ah, my Bailey and her sweet, *sweet* love words," he said dryly.

I sniffed. "I seem to remember you telling me that I smelled like shit once upon a time."

He waggled his brows, grinning over at me. "What I *didn't* tell you was that I actually love the smell of horse shit."

"*Bull* shit."

Now we were both laughing at this ridiculous conversation —which, face it, didn't feel the least bit good on my ribs—but *we were laughing* and it had cleared away the fear, freed up my lungs.

I could do this.

I could cross this bridge.

I could see what was on the other side and handle whatever may come.

Axel sensed that resolution in me, the laughter fading away, his hand still tight in mine. "Ready?"

I nodded.

He put the car into drive and took us over the bridge.

———

It was gone.

The barn. Reduced to jagged, blackened chunks. One wall still standing, the others collapsed on each other, the roof in pieces and jumbled like dominos. Data had been born in that barn. I'd bottle-fed Picard in the far stall. Cut apples and used Gramps' tools and stashed sugar cubes in my pockets. Axel had caught me when I'd fallen from the ladder, shielded me from the shards of glass when the large fluorescent lightbulb had shattered over his back.

And everything else was gone, too.

The fences I'd battled to keep in place for years. Charred and collapsed.

My herd. Out there somewhere—scared and lost or worse, dead.

The paddocks devoid of grass, of life.

But I hadn't brought myself to be able to turn to the house, to see what remained.

I needed to, but—

I kept my focus on the fields, the scorched hillsides, the broken barn and the downed fences and the paddocks that wouldn't be suited for riding for a good long while.

A warm hand on my nape.

No words. Just silent support at my side, my back.

I leaned back against Axel and slowly allowed my head to turn.

The impact took my breath away.

Gone.

There was *nothing* left except the chimney and the concrete foundation—not the porch where Axel and I had met thanks to Billie's interference, not the kitchen and family room where we'd made so many memories, not the hall and the long, narrow table of Gran's, the pictures from my childhood stacked five deep. Blackened gravel lead up to...

Nothing.

One second, I was on my feet—or one foot and one cast.

The next, my legs were giving way.

Crutches hitting the ground, my body wavering, my mind blinking out.

But then, strong, warm arms were around me, holding me up, holding me so tightly that my ribs protested. I needed it, though. Needed that bite of physical pain in order to ground me from the emotional pain.

The loss.

"Damn," I whispered, tears dripping down my cheeks.

"I'm sorry, buttercup."

"I know." Still whispering.

But *fuck*. It was *all* gone.

And I stood there, staring at the charred remains of something that had made me so freaking happy, and also so sad and so frustrated and so hopeless and like I was drowning...and none of that mattered in that moment.

Because it was gone.

I didn't know if I was grieving the loss or crying in relief, but I did know that the guilt was real.

Russet Ranch had been in my family for generations.

And now it was gone under my watch.

After I'd fought so hard to keep it, after I'd resented that fight so intensely. After I'd *loved* it so much.

The tall grass and soft moos.

The whisper of the wind and the blazing heat of the summer sun.

Gone.

All of it gone.

I stood there, leaning against the one thing that remained.

Axel.

And he was holding me tight, holding me together.

Not rushing me, letting me look my fill, needing to commit it all to memory.

Until I'd had enough.

"Can we go?" I whispered.

He nodded, but instead of bending and handing me my crutches, he carefully scooped me up and carried me to the car, tucking me inside, buckling the belt over my middle.

Then the door was closed and he disappeared.

I stared off at the hills, at the otherworldly damage, assuming he'd gone back for my crutches. Not realizing that he'd been gone for longer than that.

Not until the door behind me opened, the smell of smoke intruding.

My crutches hit the back seat.

The door closed.

He rounded the hood, climbed in through the driver's side, and then gently set something in my lap.

Surprised, my gaze drifted down, shocked by the heavy weight.

My heart squeezed tight.

It was the horseshoe Gramps and I had hung over the front door, all those years before.

TWENTY

AXEL

She'd fallen asleep less than an hour into the drive back to my apartment, and I couldn't deny that I was relieved.

She needed rest.

And I...needed the quiet, needed the break, needed the rest, too.

Bailey had fallen apart, understandably, had needed me to be her rock. I wasn't holding that against her, wouldn't ever hold it against her.

But I was riddled with fault lines.

One more impact was going to break me into pieces.

I couldn't let it.

She *needed* me.

But the lines kept appearing, kept spreading, kept threatening to shatter me.

Her house destroyed. The barn. The fields burned and the gravel scorched and...

Fuck.

How close I'd come to losing her—

A breath, my fingers clenching on the steering wheel, my vision growing just a little blurry. For a few hours, I'd managed to think about hockey, to be in the moment of winning, but book-ended on either side of that almost unreal dream were the nightmares.

The hours on the plane.

The time spent searching for her.

The smoke and heat and devastation left behind.

The people in the shelter.

The ranch—or what was left of it.

The...call that morning.

I released a shaky breath, allowed myself to glance over at her, to watch her resting peacefully, just for a moment.

Then I focused on the road ahead.

I couldn't take care of her and be broken at the same time.

So...

I needed to find a way to fill in those cracks.

I needed...to find a way to be enough for her.

I was worried that—

I wouldn't.

That I wouldn't find a way.

That I wouldn't be enough to make those nightmares in her mind and heart fade away.

"Are you okay?" Bailey asked.

I blinked, jerking my head away from the gathering of my teammates. It had started as a game night at my place to celebrate the win (though later, after the kids went to sleep, I was sure the guys would get back to partying in a more adult way). But for now, my teammates and Scarlett, along with the team's former publicist and Scar's mentor, Rebecca—were posting on social media and coordinating donations while live-streaming a *Ticket to Ride* marathon.

But people weren't just donating money online. They were also bringing supplies in person.

Because of Rebecca and Scarlett and their PR mojo. They'd sent out a few tweets, had gotten sound bites from me, from Bailey, from Billie Rose and they'd gone viral. Rebecca had coordinated getting volunteers to the Gold Mine to load container trucks she'd also somehow managed to gather. Scarlett was on the horn, finding out the biggest need for those donations and somehow also organizing local housing for those displaced by the fire.

California's landscape was designed to burn.

Hell, one species of the state tree, the Giant Sequoia, couldn't grow without fire—the seeds trapped in its tiny cones until flames dried them out enough for them to crack open. Only then would those seeds hit the forest floor, have a chance at growing into the huge California Redwoods.

Was this a useless piece of information?

Maybe.

But had I stayed up way too late researching fire and fire danger and California's climate and where it was safest for Bailey to live?

Yes.

I had.

And had basically learned that there was nowhere safe.

"Axel?"

I rubbed my forehead, stared down at the woman I loved. "Yeah, buttercup?"

Her hand rested on mine, fingers digging into the ache, massaging lightly, as though her touch might make it go away. Another day maybe it would. Today...it was just a reminder of the agony crawling through my mind, creating the dissonance that had me firmly in its grip. "I think you need to go lie down," she murmured.

No.

I needed to stay awake.

Needed to make sure that this all went okay, that Bailey was okay.

If I slept and something happened and—

"Honey." Her hand slid down, rested on my shoulder. "You're exhausted."

I'd driven up to River's Bend and back down that morning and afternoon, we'd spent time in the shelter, at her ranch. I'd played late into the night the previous evening, had spent a frantic day and night and day searching for her, worrying about her, thinking I was going to lose her.

So, yeah, I was exhausted.

But I could look after the woman I loved.

I *needed* to look after the woman I loved.

I—

Her hand slid down to rest on my chest, over my heart. It was pounding, thumping against my ribs. "Axel, honey, you—"

I shook my head, yanked myself firmly out of my mind. "I'm fine, buttercup." I glanced at the clock, registered the time, realized I'd fucked up. Again. "Let me get your meds. You need to have your next dose." Late. It was late.

I had one fucking job.

She needed the medicine on time, needed the antibiotics to make sure she healed.

Bailey dropped her hand from my chest, reached for her crutches. "Oh. Right. I forgot. I'll get 'em."

My feet were under me before she could get up. "Stay there. I'll grab them." Then I was moving into the kitchen, bypassing the crew on the couches, the board with colorful train tracks laid out in front of them, and going to the stack of discharge papers, the bottles of antibiotics and pain medicine. Opening them, shaking out the proper dose, filling a cup of water for her.

I needed to take better care of her.

I'd almost lost her.

I'd *almost* lost her.

Pulse thudding in my ears, I dropped my hands onto the counter, squeezed my eyes tightly closed.

"You need to give yourself some grace."

My lids flew open, and I straightened, not letting my eyes go to Brit's. I hadn't heard her move up next to me, but I knew she would see too much if I *did* look at her.

"Axel."

Her hand covered mine on the counter, holding it tightly.

I could feel the pressure, but it wasn't warm, wasn't totally connecting.

Maybe that might have worried me on a normal day.

But life hadn't been all that normal of late.

"I'm fine," I said, slipping my hand free, turning toward the loaf of bread. Bailey needed to eat something with the pain meds, otherwise it might upset her stomach.

Two slices of bread in the toaster.

Butter out of the fridge. Cinnamon and sugar—her go to—out of the cabinet.

Knife. Plate.

Brit still leaning against the counter.

My eyes still determinedly kept away.

"Don't shut her out."

I blinked and this time my gaze slid to Brit's, unable to keep it away, and what I saw punched me right in the gut.

Pain. Hers.

Pain from past experience.

Pain from a woman who was so tough and self-assured and confident that it almost seemed like she *couldn't* be hurt.

"Brit," I murmured.

Her mouth tipped up, that pain fading, her normal unflappable self making a reappearance. "That hurts us," she whispered. "Not being able to help the men we love sort out their heads."

My hand shot out, gripped hers. "You and Stefan—"

"We're fine." She smiled. "But last year..." A shake of her head.

"He was dealing with some stuff, and him not talking to me, shutting me out made me feel like shit."

I hated that she'd felt that way but was glad it was an old hurt, that she and Stefan were past it.

"You guys want to take care of us, protect us. But shutting us out of what's in your heart and head isn't that."

I inhaled.

Bailey didn't want to know what was in my head.

Hell, right now it wasn't *safe* for her to know what was in it.

It wasn't protection or care or—

The toast popped up.

Brit turned her hand over, gripped mine when I started to pull away. "Are you hearing me?"

I was...but, for once, her advice didn't apply to my life.

I wasn't going to tell her that, though.

I just nodded. "I'm hearing you." I tugged my hand free, buttered the bread. A glance up. "I'm hearing you," I repeated more firmly when she didn't move away.

Hearing, yes.

Just not going to listen.

Brit knew a lot, had advised me plenty over the last months.

I trusted her judgment.

Just not in this.

Bailey didn't need to know this.

Not now.

Maybe not ever.

Twenty-One

BAILEY

He wasn't touching her.

He wasn't sleeping.

Or if he *was* sleeping, it was barely more than an hour or two at a time.

He was doing a good job of faking it, and I'd been in so much pain, so tired from everything that it had taken me a solid week to realize how far gone he was.

Now the pain was better—my ribs were feeling better, the stitches had come out, the bruises had faded.

My leg barely hurt—the cast more of an irritation and the actual break wasn't bothering me. Though, the crutches weren't more of an irritation. They were *definitely* one.

Mostly because my armpits were angry anytime I was using them.

But considering I'd barely had to get out of bed, or off the couch, they were far from as bad as they could have been.

Because Axel had hardly let me use the toilet, let alone going anywhere where I might be tired out. Not without a fight anyway.

And I'd fought.

I was me, so *of course* I had.

In the last two weeks, we'd been back up to River's Bend several times, helping at the shelter, but the last time we'd been there it had almost been empty. With the fire contained and slowly burning—and being put—out, people had either been able to go home or had been moved into more permanent temporary housing.

An oxymoron. But people couldn't live permanently in a large, open gymnasium.

They needed their own space and privacy and a little bit of normalcy returning.

The Gold had helped with that—mainly Rebecca and Scarlett, the team's publicist. They'd managed to keep the fire in the news, to coordinate donations, to link available housing with people in need.

Because it wasn't just River's Bend—though it had the biggest need in the aftermath of this fire—other small towns had been damaged, their residents needing help.

People were getting it.

Not Axel though.

He was still off.

And I was trying to be understanding, trying to be patient, but swear to Christ, the man was shutting me out tighter than a vault at a high security secret government organization. I was attempting to give him that time, knowing that it had been traumatic for the both of us.

But he wasn't talking to me, wasn't touching me, except in a distant medical way, as though constantly assessing my injuries. He was barely looking at me, and he certainly didn't appear to notice that I was getting better.

Hell, half the time I felt like he wasn't even *seeing* me.

It was like he was still back out in the woods, in the town, searching desperately for me.

What did I do with that?

What *could* I do with that?

Other than to just be here and be patient and try to get better, to show him I was here and safe. But as the days went on and he turned into more of a zombie, every night I went to sleep with him still and awake beside me and in the morning, I woke up with him still and awake and not touching me.

I wanted him to touch me.

I wanted him to unfreeze.

I just...had no idea how to make that happen, and everyone had more than enough on their plates—you know, with rebuilding a town and finding people places to live and coordinating supply drops and all.

Meanwhile, I was stuck here, wanting to help but not able to do much.

And the only thing I could potentially help—namely sorting Axel's head out—I was failing miserably at.

His phone rang, and he looked at the screen, swiped as though he was supremely hesitant—and maybe he was. I'd gotten my replacement cell just a few days before, and it had been ringing off the hook with media requests.

He was certainly being hit up even more frequently—though Olivia, his agent, was fielding most of the offers.

Now, though, he listened for a moment, body going statue stiff, then hung up on the caller.

Tapping a few buttons, presumably blocking the call.

Considering I'd gotten more than a few of *those* types of callers too, I understood the need to block them.

We were living in strange, strange times.

I sighed.

"What?" He'd pushed to his feet, hustled into the bedroom before I'd even fully processed that I'd made a noise at all. I'd told him I was going to rest, but really, I'd been thinking, trying and failing to come up with a way to break through.

Impossible when he was both distant and so close I couldn't wind up to punch through.

"Nothing, honey," I said.

He stopped in the doorway.

A few days ago, he'd stopped a few feet from the bed.

Before that it had been the edge of the bed.

Before *that* he'd been in bed with me.

A slow retraction. A slow walling over.

I was trying not to take it personally.

Trying not to wonder if that he was having second thoughts about us.

"What?" he asked again, still from the doorway.

My gaze drifted to the window, to the tall buildings outside it, to the fog and the busy city beyond the glass. I wanted to be out there.

But also, I wanted to be out amongst the tall grass, riding on Data's back, feeling the cool, fresh air on my face, the sun tightening the skin on my cheeks. I wanted to be back a few weeks, to what Axel and I were then. Not what were now, this weird in between, like both of us were afraid to take a breath.

"Buttercup, *what?*"

And suddenly, the in between we'd been existing in constricted tightly around me, making my lungs feel like I was back in those smokey woods, making me feel like I couldn't breathe.

Two weeks of this.

Two weeks of this slowly getting worse.

It was too much like what I'd had with Colt, good being slowly poisoned until it was untenable, until it was something I couldn't handle, until it smothered and sucked my life out of me and turned me into someone I didn't recognize.

Axel wasn't Colt.

Not even close.

Colt was a fucking monster, and Axel was good down to his core.

But I still wasn't going to let us, let our relationship and love and connection die by inches.

"What?" I asked, turning to face him, seeing that he'd taken another step toward me.

Which pissed me off.

Because there were still at least ten more between us.

We weren't supposed to be separate. We were supposed to be together. I'd fought to stay alive, fought to get to him. Just like he'd fought to find me, fought to make sure I stayed alive.

"*What?*" I asked again. "You're seriously asking me that?"

He blinked.

"Who was on the phone?"

His teeth clicked together.

"What aren't you telling me?"

Because there was something eating at him and maybe it was all the calls—but then again, the solution to that was easy and started and ended with turning the damned thing off—but though the nasty phone calls weren't entirely pleasant—I could attest to that—I didn't think that was the right explanation.

Things were foggy from exhaustion and pain pills, but I thought he'd been off before then.

He'd been off from the moment we'd gone up to the ranch?

From the morning after the game?

I rubbed my forehead.

I didn't know precisely. But he'd been different from that day forward.

"Are you hurting?" he asked, turning toward the kitchen. "I can get your—"

"*Stop.*"

His expression went wounded.

Probably because I was snapping at him. Okay, that wasn't exactly true. I was pretty much yelling at him. Which made me an asshole, I knew. Especially after all he'd done for me.

"You're hurting," he said.

A step away from me.

And fucking hell. But, dammit, I was done with this.

Done.

"Stop *right* there."

Something about my tone clearly got through because he stopped, slowly spun back to face me. "Buttercup."

"*What* is going on in your head?"

His face clouded over.

"No," I said. "Axel. Honey. You *need* to tell me what's going on in your head."

"I'm fine."

I laughed and, yeah, it was more than a little brittle. "*That's* what you're going with?"

He frowned, brows dragged together into a tight vee. "What are you talking about?"

"You're not sleeping." I threw up a hand, palm out, cutting off the protest before it passed his lips. "You're hardly eating. You jump when I breathe or sigh or wince or move. But somehow, you're doing all that without actually touching to me or talking to me or *looking* at me."

"In fairness"—he crossed his arms, leaned back against the doorframe—"I've touched you plenty."

"To help me shower or get into the car or bed or get dressed. All of which I appreciate," I added. "My recovery would have been a lot harder without you."

"So what's the problem?"

His body language was telling me to back off, to not press this.

But I wasn't that woman anymore.

I'd let this slide for two weeks. I couldn't let the gulf between us continue to grow.

"The problem is you're not *yourself*," I whispered. "Ever since we went up to River's Bend you haven't been the Axel I know."

"I've been—"

"Please don't make a quick excuse," I said, hurt blooming in my chest, bleeding over into my tone. "Please just stop and think and *talk* to me."

His shoulders rose and fell on a breath. He pushed up off the doorframe, took a step farther into the bedroom, took a step toward me.

I braced, ready to hear whatever it was he was going to tell me.

But I didn't *get* to hear it.

Because he spun on his heel and left the room.

"Ax—"

The front door opened.

Closed.

Twenty-Two

Axel

I leaned back against the closed front door, my phone's case creaking in one hand, my keys clutched tight enough to hurt my palm in the other.

My heart was pounding, sweat dripping down my spine, my lungs working desperately to modulate my breathing.

I couldn't.

I *couldn't*.

"Fuck," I whispered, eyes sliding closed, trying to smother the panic. "*Fuck.*"

A thump from inside the apartment, the sound of Bailey crutching her way toward me following a few seconds later.

That had me pushing off the door, my eyes snapping open.

Had me heading for the stairs, bypassing the elevator because I couldn't wait for it, couldn't risk Bailey catching up.

I needed to go.

I needed space.

I needed to *breathe*.

Yanking open the door that led to the stairwell, I released a sigh of relief when I found it empty. Then I was moving down the stairs, boots pounding on the treads.

Down. Down. Down.

Bursting out into the parking garage, moving out through the ugly concrete space.

Then onto the street.

I got a few looks, but it was San Francisco. Weird shit happened all the time, so my bursting out of the garage didn't garner more than couple of sideways glances before people were going about their business.

Lucky for me, considering the news coverage that had been trailing the team of late.

The last thing I wanted to was to have to put on a happy face for a fan...and the last thing I *would* do was ruin someone else's night by being an asshole.

That was the old Axel.

I was...

Enough.

Inhaling sharply, I turned off the busier street and down one that was quieter, darker, that fit my mood...just as my phone buzzed.

I love you.

Three words from the woman who held my heart and was tearing it to shreds at the same time.

"Think, Axel," I muttered, drawing to a stop, resting my fists against the graffitied wall. "*Think.*"

The news had turned me into a hero.

Those same forces would love to tear me down.

One word would set the bloodhounds down the trail and then I'd be in pieces. Something I could survive—I'd done it before. But the hounds wouldn't stop with just me. They'd go after the team and Bailey and—

I couldn't let them do that.

I couldn't let *her* do it.

So I had to find a way to stop her, even if—

I love you. YOU, Axel. I don't know what's going on in your mind, but I'm here to listen.

I turned my cell away, not wanting to see those words on the screen.

I *couldn't* see them.

But when my cell buzzed again, I flipped it over again, read the message from Bailey anyway.

And I'm not going to run from whatever demons are chasing you.

"Fuck," I whispered then slammed my fists against the wall. "*Think.*"

Bailey didn't text again, and though I was disappointed, I wasn't surprised. I hadn't replied to her, hadn't acknowledged the words that meant too much. I'd left her when she was injured and—

"Think," I whispered again, shoving my cell back into my pocket, cutting the useless spiraling off. I had to shut it down, shut it all down. To focus on the problem at hand. To come up with a solution that wouldn't ruin everything and slice away the only bit of happiness I'd ever truly allowed myself.

I started walking again, mind turning over the problem.

Studying it from every angle I could think of.

And not finding a solution that would protect her, protect them, not without exposing every single vulnerability that I'd long buried.

Because if I gave in to the threat, it would never stop.

She would never stop.

———

I should have stayed away longer.

I knew the risk of going back to the apartment.

But it hadn't been a conscious decision to go back, not really.

My feet had just...led me up to the apartment.

In through the door, closing and locking it behind me.

Boots off.

Cell on the counter. Jacket on the hook.

And my eyes hitting Bailey's, who was sitting on the couch, waiting for me.

There was a plate in front of her, the remnants of a sandwich on its plain gray surface. An open bottle of beer sitting on a coaster next to it, something I would have gotten on her about, if not for the fact that she'd been refusing to take the pain medicine for near on a week now.

But, pain medicine or not, she'd still had to make herself dinner, and that couldn't have been easy with the crutches, with the unwieldy cast, with the ribs she said weren't bothering her but still made her wince when she moved too quickly or twisted to the side.

Guilt.

Fuck, it was a dagger-wielding bitch, stabbing me over and over and *over* again.

My gaze dropped from the warm chocolate of hers, dragged over the gray-tinted hardwood floor, searching the pattern of woodgrain that would distract me from the repeated impact of that remorse.

Fucking this up.

Fucking *all* of this up.

"I'm good at flying off the handle, rushing forward and not thinking things through." Her voice was gentle, and that was somehow more abrasive, more painful than if she'd been yelling again. *That* I'd deserved. The gentle...it felt like a kick to the teeth.

Not for me.

Not with what I might lay at her feet.

"But *you're* good at closing everyone out and getting lost in your pain," she murmured. "Only"—a breath, as though she were bracing herself—"It's not hiding behind alcohol and sex this time."

My gaze flew up to hers.

"Instead, you're hiding behind taking care of me."

I sucked in a breath.

"And"—still gentle—"I'm happy to be that shield."

My lungs compressed silently, the air sliding out in a rapid silent shot. "But only if you let me inside *yours*."

Now my lungs compressed for another reason, one completely different and stifling.

I *couldn't* let her in.

That was fucking laughable.

"Buttercup."

She held up a palm. "Not an ultimatum. Just...something I need you to think about and take seriously."

I froze. "I love you."

Her smile was small...and a little sad. "I know." A whisper. "Which is why it's *not* an ultimatum."

But the unspoken threat beneath that statement was clear.

It could easily become one.

And it would be my fault.

My fault.

I could ruin the best thing in my life so, so easily.

That sent the dagger-wielding regret bitch stabbing away again, but even though each wound left me bleeding even more heavily, I didn't see how I could dump this on Bailey's lap. Not when I hadn't even been able to wrap my own head around it, hadn't come up with a plan, a way to make things better, hadn't figured out how to protect her.

So, I dealt with something else she'd brought up.

"You said I hadn't touched you."

Her chin came up slightly, the slightest bit of defensiveness in her posture, as though she expected him to deny that statement. "You haven't," she said. "Not like how a man should touch his woman."

I got the distinction. Because I'd touched her. Of course, I had.

But it had all been helping her—into the shower, getting dressed, steadying her when she wobbled. It was care, just not for her heart and soul.

Because *my* heart and soul hadn't been able to take it.

Not since the call.

Not since *seeing* how close I had come to losing her, knowing that the call might result in that anyway.

So no, I hadn't touched her as I should.

Not since my head had gotten well and totally fucked up.

"Not since we got back from the ranch that first time." Her voice shook just the slightest bit, making me feel like an even bigger asshole.

Congrats, Axel.

Asshole to the world.

Asshole to the woman you love.

"You haven't touched me, honey, and I don't know how to make it feel like you can, how to break through."

More voice shaking.

More dagger stabs.

More regret welding itself to my cells.

I had to give her something.

I had to at least give her part of the truth.

So, I did.

I walked across the room, knelt at her feet and *gave*.

"I haven't touched you because I need you so badly that I'm afraid I'll hurt you."

Twenty-Three

I inhaled sharply enough to have my still healing ribs protesting.

I haven't touched you because I need you so badly that I'm afraid I'll hurt you.

This man.

What he did to me.

What *I* was doing to him.

Fuck.

His eyes were haunted. His jaw taut. His hands clenched into fists that were resting on my thighs. It was those fists that undid me. That unfroze me.

That had me giving in to what my body and heart needed.

Leaning forward, I wrapped my arms around Axel's wide shoulders and hauled him against me, my lips finding his.

For one second, they were unmoving against mine.

Then he was in motion, and the man I loved, the man who'd been able to handle my body like it was a puck on his stick, easy to manipulate, to make it do what he wanted, to push it over the line and in the goal, was back.

He was excellent at getting me over the line.

So good that he often left me as a puddle of goo who could barely lift an arm.

But I didn't want to be goo, didn't want to be pleasured within an inch of my life.

Okay, I *did* want that.

But I needed to be right here with him more.

Something that was made immeasurably more difficult after he'd snapped out of his shock and his tongue slipped between my lips, tangling with mine. The man could *kiss*. The man knew exactly when to go fast and when to slow things down...*way* down until my brain went fuzzy and my body went molten and...

Oh yeah, I was ready for him to sweep me up into his arms, ready for me to carry him to the bedroom and lay me on top of the comforter.

I was ready for my shirt to disappear—*poof, look at it go*—over my head.

I was ready for him to come over the top of me, for him to give me some of his weight. Not too much, because he was Axel and he was aware of my body, of what still hurt, what was still healing.

But, oh man, did I like the feel of his body gently nudging my thighs apart, his torso pressing to mine. His lips, his teeth, his tongue dragging over my skin.

Goosebumps on my flesh.

Heat in my belly, drifting lower.

Just like his mouth.

I wasn't wearing a bra, had lost that the moment I'd traded in my daytime sweats for my nighttime sweats (that being a plain black cotton pair he'd loaned me that I could get over my cast and still tie around my waist for a patterned pair that Brit had bought me with adorable abominable snowmen that had wide legs and an elastic waist). Being braless was a perk in most instances, but it was especially one in that moment because it meant that Axel was free to slide his lips over my collarbones, down over the tops of my breasts.

A flick of his tongue between them, the days old growth of his beard tickling my skin, causing my nipples to bead tightly.

I arched up, instinctively seeking his mouth, desperate for the slight rasp of his tongue, for the suction of his lips.

He didn't disappoint, didn't make me wait.

Just sucked one taut bud and did it hard and deep.

I gasped, his name tumbling off my tongue, my free leg wrapping around his waist, pelvis arching, hips seeking purchase. I needed hard. I needed *in*. It had been too long without Axel stretching me wide, without his thick cock pressing home, without his body making mine sing.

Teeth on my skin, a rough palm on my ribcage, dragging up, cupping one breast as he went and worked my other one with his mouth.

I'd lost control.

I was slowly turning into a pile of goo.

Which wasn't what I wanted, wasn't what he needed, but every time I tried to focus, to remember what it *was* that I wanted (because what he was doing was really, really nice), to recall what he needed, Axel worked his magic.

Goo.

That puck being drawn closer and closer to the goal line.

Which was the moment that my mind wrenched to full attention.

"No!" I said, pushing his head back, his mouth pulling on my nipple for one extra tug before he released me.

And blinked, eyes out of focus, red tinting the edges of his cheeks. "Did I hurt you?" he rasped.

No.

He'd been pleasuring me into goo.

He'd been giving, but not taking, not accepting *my* care.

"No, honey," I murmured. "You didn't hurt me."

"Then—"

"I want you," I said, cupping his jaw. "But I also want you with me. This"—I tapped his chest, just above his heart—"and this"— his temple—"need to be with me, too."

Axel was stiff above me, his fingers clenched into fists again.

But worse, his blue eyes were filled with hurt.

"I'm with you," he said. "I'd never think of anyone but you while we—"

Fuck.

That wasn't what I'd meant.

I mean, okay, it kind of *was* what I'd meant. I just...needed to make sure he wasn't trying to distract me with sex, wasn't using it to keep me at a distance.

Wasn't leaving me the object to be pleasured and cared for while he himself was able to keep his distance because he was in control.

"I know."

His eyes didn't clear.

"Honey, *I know.* I just..." A breath. "I need you to go a little slower, to let me touch you, too, okay? It's been a while for us and I-I—"

His face softened. "I'm rushing you."

"Being wanted by my sexy hockey player isn't a bad thing." I leaned up, pressed a kiss to his cheek. "I just...be here *with* me, yeah? Don't take over."

Give me a little.

Don't wall me off and make this just about getting off.

Don't keep your distance and make me feel like this doesn't mean as much to you as it does to me.

Us.

I needed for this time together to bring us back to *us.*

His knuckles brushed over my cheek, the ghost of a cocky

smile on his mouth. And, fuck, that smile was such an *Axel Smile* that relief rushed through me.

Maybe this was truly all that was the matter.

Maybe he *was* scared of hurting me, scared of going too fast and wanting me too much (and didn't that feel good?). Maybe it was...

Simple.

Maybe the answer was just something simple.

We let each other back in this way. We find our way back to us.

"I know it hasn't been *that* long since I've been inside you, buttercup. Have you forgotten?"

Ho, mama.

"Forgotten what?" I asked softly.

His fingers trailing over my sternum, down my belly, drifting beneath the waistband of my sweats.

"Forgotten how good it feels when I take over." A nip to my jaw. "Forgotten that you *like* it when I take over."

I did like it.

I liked it very, very much.

But...*focus woman!*

Which was why I summoned my strength and pushed him. Rolling to my side, taking him with me until our bodies were facing each other. I knew he'd let me press him back, that he was too heavy for me to shift him if he didn't want to go. I still took advantage of the shift in our positions, sliding down, glad there was no footboard on the bed because the damned cast was unwieldy.

I managed to get down the mattress, to get *me* down the mattress.

Until my nose was pressed just above the waistband of his jeans.

My lips twitched in what I presumed was a very Axel-like smile.

Because *this* was exactly where I was desperate to be.

TWENTY-FOUR

AXEL

Her fingers were...
Oh sweet baby Jesus.
They were brushing the top of my cock.

"Bailey—"

Flick.

The button on my jeans popped open.

Her fingers became her palm *and* fingers slipping beneath my underwear, wrapping around my dick, squeezing tightly enough that I saw fucking black.

I wanted to flip us over and stroke into her until we both found oblivion.

I wanted to take over, to make sure that we were both lost in pleasure, to not think about everything that had gone wrong and everything I was holding back.

I wanted—

Her mouth joined her hand and then I wasn't thinking about what I wanted to do or desperate to take over.

I was in taut, wet heat. There was suction. There was tongue moving along my shaft, flicking over my head, over the sensitive spot right near the tip.

Tight.

Slick.

Then she did something with her hands and tongue and...*oh fucking hell*. My cock bobbed against the back of her throat and...

Shit.

She swallowed me down, her lips brushing against my pelvis, her mouth stretched wide, her eyes a little damp as though she'd taken me too deep.

But she didn't stop.

And yeah, I guess I was still that asshole, because I didn't stop her.

Because I let her inch forward, her nose bumping against me, my cock down her throat.

And just that quickly I was three strokes—maybe less—away from exploding.

"*Bailey.*"

"Mmm."

Oh *fuck*. That was...making it seem like it would take less than three strokes to make me come. I was...

Milliseconds away from it.

"Buttercup, you need—"

She gripped me tighter.

My eyes rolled back. My hips arched up, taking me deeper. She coughed, and I felt like the biggest dickhead on the planet, even more so when tears slid out from the corners of her eyes, but she didn't stop.

And neither did I.

My balls tightened.

Pleasure coiled at the base of my spine and...

I came.

Another cough, but when I would have pulled back, she swallowed me down, swallowed the hot jets of my release, wringing me dry.

One second, I was safe and sheltered and *separate.*

And the next, I was safe and sheltered and held by the woman who loved me.

A long, slow withdrawal, her tongue darting out to the corners of that pink, swollen mouth. Someone had tied concrete blocks to my wrists, to my ankles, my head, I was so weak and limp with pleasure.

My cock, though, wasn't limp.

It was somehow still hard, still bobbing like a radar detector to the woman who owned it.

Bailey had wriggled up so that our faces were equal and drew a long, slow hand along my chest, my stomach. "Normally, I'd climb on top and take care of you all submissive with pleasure," she murmured, her lips turned up at the edges, the flushed and puffy flesh making me want to slip my cock between them again. "But," she whispered, one finger trailing over the sensitive head of my dick, "I don't think I can manage that with the cast."

The chains holding the concrete blocks to me snapped, and the heavy weights flew away.

Then my hands were beneath her, shifting her on the bed, making sure her head hit the pillows and not the hard wooden frame.

Her sweats were tossed over the side of the mattress a second later, after making certain to carefully draw them down over her cast.

Then she was gloriously naked.

Mouth swollen, breasts pinkened from the rough bristles of my beard.

More assholeness because I should have cared, should have shaved so as not to mark up her pretty, pretty skin.

But...

I liked her marked up.

I liked her *mine*.

Then I was crawling between her legs, pressing her uninjured leg out to the side, making room for my shoulders, my mouth.

I was going to make this pussy mine, too.

A long, rough flick of my tongue, slicking up from her entrance to circle the bundle of nerves of her clit. Her slick folds were sensitive and I made sure to use my knowledge of her body, of all of special spots that made her melt for me.

Just for me.

Only for me.

Because she was *mine*.

No quarter on that fact, even if the truth of what I was keeping from her might tear us apart.

She was mine.

And I wasn't letting her go.

That lack of quarter meant that I showed no mercy on her pussy, on her body. My tongue working against her, making her writhe and cry out my name, making her mine, branding her soul.

Mine. Mine. Mine.

She'd burst through the barriers I'd tried to erect, brought out the man who needed someone to be his. There was no going back, not when she'd owned my heart from the moment she'd tipped back her cowboy hat and pointed a shotgun at me.

A finger through that slick heat, pressing in.

"No," she murmured, head thrashing on the pillow. "I want *you* inside me."

No quarter here either, not as her pussy clamped tightly around the digit, sending that pattern of convulsions straight to my cock.

Mine. Mine. Mine.

But I'd see her fall apart first, see her shatter so I could pick up the pieces.

Like she'd done for me.

Leaning up, I dragged the rough stubble of my beard over her labia, latched my lips around her clit, sucked hard.

"Axel!"

Yeah, the asshole in me liked the way my name sounded as she screamed it.

I was the man who loved her, not willing to accept any other sign of her need, of her pleasure, of her desire for me.

I kept sucking, kept stroking that finger in and out.

Added another despite my cock throbbing, angry at being denied all that tight, wet heat.

Luckily, it didn't need to be denied for long.

Because then she was coming on my lips, my tongue, my fingers.

I slipped from her clenching pussy, came up her body, and thrust inside, capturing her gasp on my tongue.

I tasted myself on her, knew she could probably taste the same, and it only served to drive me closer to the edge. I stroked into her, slow and steady at first, drawing out the pleasure of her orgasm, then faster when she wrapped her good leg around me, arched her hips so that I slipped deeper.

A jolt through my belly, my cock, signaling that my control was fucking bullshit, that I was one second away from forgetting everything—every healing wound and bone and bruise—and just pounding into her.

Something she knew apparently.

Because she tore her mouth from mine, gaze pinning me in place.

"Everything, honey," she murmured, palm coming to my cheek. "I'll always want every part of you."

I shuddered.

Her lips parted, eyes going heavy-lidded, pussy tightening around me.

But still she repeated, "Everything."

And it was that *everything* that finally shattered me.

———

"Now, honey," she whispered, maybe minutes, maybe an eternity, later, our breaths still coming quickly, her sexy body covered in a fine sheen of sweat from the orgasm I'd led us both to those minutes, or maybe that eternity ago. "Now," she said again, "you need to tell me what's going on in that head of yours."

I had a choice.

It was clear as day now, obvious in this moment, after what we'd just shared.

I could keep building walls, keep trying to protect her, keep finding ways to keep her out.

But she wasn't leaving.

And...I was hurting her. Hurting the woman I loved by making her continue to have to shove through those barriers.

I worried—which was why I'd held this all so close—that this truth would hurt her.

But now I had to make a choice.

Did *I* hurt her?

Or did my past?

I stared into her gorgeous brown eyes.

And I knew that this would be a case of both.

Twenty-Five

Bailey

The look in his eyes told me two things.

One, he was finally going to share what had been tearing him up these last couple of weeks.

Two, it was going to flay me to the bone.

For a moment, panic gripped me tightly enough to steal my breath, to send my pulse skittering, a cold sweat gathering between my shoulder blades. But then I managed to fill myself with steel, with focus.

I loved this man with every cell in my body, every fiber in my being, every breath that carried oxygen to my blood and brain and all the other pertinent parts.

I would take whatever burden he was shouldering, and I *wouldn't* collapse beneath the weight.

We'd been through too much, had come too far.

Lungs screaming from the lack of oxygen, I didn't let them fill quickly, didn't allow him to see what the look in his eyes did to me, the sheer terror in my belly. Instead, I released my hold on them slowly, carefully, breathing gently as I'd done in the days after I'd left the hospital, easing my aching ribs back to full use.

They were still sore, didn't like that I'd been holding my breath, but they weren't anything like the agony in those first few days.

But the slow, steady breath allowed the oxygen to hit my system, helped me to breathe more easily, to ease away the panic and even out my pulse. The sweat would dry into the comforter, into my skin, both of which were already covered in their fair share of dirty from the events of the previous thirty minutes.

From *our* little bit of dirty that had unlocked my man.

Finally.

I inhaled again, released it just as slowly.

Then I nodded, sat up, and pulled the blanket that had been folded neatly and spread out along the bottom of the mattress and was now rucked up into a ball of fabric, over my lap. "I'm ready."

He shifted a few pillows behind me, tucking them so that I would be comfortable—always looking after me, always protecting me. Then he straightened and his fingers brushed over my cheek as his lids slid closed. A heartbeat later, they were opening again and instead of agony in the piercing blue depths, there was resignation and determination and caution.

"Hold on," he whispered, and then he was shifting off the bed, moving to one of the nightstands, upon which he'd carefully propped Gramps's horseshoe against the lamp. He opened to the top drawer, reaching inside and pulling out a large manila envelope.

He handed it to me.

"The morning after we won the Cup, I got a phone call from my mother."

I braced.

"She threatened to expose me to the new management on the team, to the media if I didn't pay her off."

My rage was a taut, coiled beast, ready to lash out at the piece of shit that was Axel's mother. God, she'd already done so much harm to him, and now she was going to do more, going to make it so that his life was even harder.

For money?

The envelope made a crinkling sound in my hands, but I forced myself to find my control before I crushed it. I didn't know what it was, didn't know how it fit in to the pieces Axel was sharing, but I wouldn't destroy it.

Not yet, anyway.

Carefully, I set it on my casted thigh, one hand going to my hip, clenching the knitted material of the throw, the other finding his. "The team—"

"Would stand by me," he whispered. "I know that." His chin dropped to his chest, and he inhaled, let it out slowly. Then his head came up again. "But how can I ask them to?"

I squeezed his fingers. "Because you would do that same."

His eyes on mine, silence heavy and taut.

I waited for him to say something to dispute that fact, prepared to argue because he and I both knew that it would be a lie and I was ready to take him to the proverbial mat if he tried to pass that bullshit over on me.

I knew him.

Knew him.

Once he had made a place for someone in his heart, once he'd let someone in, there were no outs. And if someone was lucky enough to have his love and respect and loyalty, no sane person would ever want to. Could he be abrasive and a bit prickly? Yes. Had I thought him more than a bit of an asshole before I'd truly understood what was beneath that jerky shield? Absolutely. But it *was* a shield. And he'd been protecting himself.

And I knew more than a little bit about protecting myself by being a porcupine.

I'd made a life out of it until Billie Rose had intervened.

The thought of naked Axel and handcuffs and my fury at

finding him on a porch that no longer existed made me both want to smile and cry at the same time.

I held both back.

He needed something else from me in this moment.

He needed steady and calm.

And braced.

"Yes," he whispered. "I would protect them with everything I could." A beat. "Which is why I was trying to handle this on my own."

He might have been able to—he was capable of so much—if not for the fact that I knew him, that we were living together, that I could feel his hurt like it was my own. Because we *were* together, he couldn't just shove everything down and wall me off.

I would know—*knew.*

So I wouldn't let him.

"I didn't want my mom to taint what I'd done, what we have." He glanced away from me, out the window, out to the bright lights of the city. "But she did anyway."

My lips parted, ready to dispute that, to argue that she would only have power if he gave it to her.

But that wasn't true, was it?

Sometimes the people in our lives exerted their power, their influence, without effort, those pathways built through childhood or adulthood or through friendship or love so ingrained that it was impossible to shut them out.

It was like trying to stop a big rig with just a simple plastic barrier gate.

They were so powerful, so big, so *heavy* that they would barrel right through.

Unless there was enough steel and concrete to bring the huge weight to a halt.

I understood that because I'd built walls that Axel had just waltzed around, had found an unlocked door in that huge expanse of steel and concrete and rebar and just strolled through. I also understood because, sometimes, no matter how thick the wall, it wouldn't be strong enough.

That pathway would still exist.

Like it did for my parents.

Even though I'd finally stood up to them, finally erected strong enough barriers so they couldn't hurt me any longer, we were still connected in ways that maybe couldn't be undone.

No contact didn't mean no power.

(Of course, with my ex, no contact meant no *fucking* contact and luckily, Colt had gotten the memo to leave me the fuck alone).

As for my parents, I hated them and yet part of me still loved them, still wanted them to wake up and be different.

And even though Axel's mom hadn't been much of one, had spent most of his childhood drunk and fucking her way through his friend's dads, through his coaches, through the scouts and people who might help him achieve his goal of making it to the NHL, that love and yearning of a child for a parent didn't ever really go away.

I knew because I'd lived that.

No stability, bounced from place to place, not knowing when the ties of my friendships might be erased, when I'd have to leave behind a prized possession because we had to leave quickly to avoid the police or an irate landlord. Not wanting to connect with teachers, to make a huge effort to be a student they'd remember.

Because who knew how long I would be there?

But I still ached with a desire to have a family like the one Billie Rose had.

Supportive parents who loved her, a stable house, friends at school, in town.

It was why my time in River's Bend with Gramps and Gran had meant so much.

But Axel hadn't had that.

Though, maybe, he'd found something *like* it with hockey.

Perhaps, that was why he'd worked so hard to find ways to play, even without the support of his mom.

Later, I'd ask him.

Now, I needed to deal with the agony creeping back into his expression.

Releasing the fisted bit of blanket, I leaned forward and rested my hand on his chest, rested it over that big, beautiful, *wounded* heart.

"What did she do, honey?"

He lungs shuddered, but he just caught my hand and brought it to the envelope.

Twenty-Six

Axel

"Read it," I managed to rasp out, my heart in my throat, stifling any further words that wanted to escape, blocking out the explanation that I wanted to give her.

The *warning*.

Her fingers shook as she reached for the envelope, turning it over and opening the flap.

Mine had shaken in very much the same way when I'd received it, received the final bit of proof that had shown beyond any doubt that my mother wasn't lying.

Not about this, anyway.

The sheaf of papers sliding out was a mere whisper of sound.

But it was also somehow more, almost gunshot loud in the quiet that had fallen between us. Now, my breaths increased in speed, in volume, joining the noise in a grating report that prickled down my spine.

I couldn't manage to slow them, though, not when Bailey had dropped her gaze to the papers.

I watched her eyes move across the page, her brows drawing

together, probably trying to make sense of the first paper in the stack.

It was a medical report.

It *was* a DNA report, generated from a sample Pascal had surreptitiously collected for me and my own saliva.

But because it had come straight from a lab, it was filled with a lot of scientific mumbo jumbo.

She reached the bottom, that frown still in place, but then she was flipping to the next page, and I knew, *knew* that if she hadn't been certain of what she'd been reading on the first piece of paper that the second would make it crystal clear.

Because it was a picture.

Of a boy.

Who had my eyes.

Who was mine based on that DNA report.

Her gasp punched through the numb that was threatening to settle over me, striking my heart with the force of a bullet. This time the papers crinkled as she flipped back to the first page, gaze flying over the words. Her mouth dropped open.

Another flip. Back to the picture.

Then to the remaining pages in the packet.

Pascal's team had done a thorough job. There was a birth certificate that listed me as the father, more pictures of him, of *my son* at school, with his mother at the park, her financial records, even a photograph of him at his birthday party.

Five.

He was five.

He was mine.

And he didn't know me. I was as absent as my own father had been. My throat went tight all over again, the guilt tearing me up, slicing me to ribbons.

"I'd gone home," I whispered, staring at the stitching of the comforter. "I'd gone home after I'd been bumped down into the minors. My mom wanted money, and I was miserable, wanted to punish myself for trusting her, for trusting myself. I-I—don't really remember much of that weekend. I gave her the money but vowed it would be the last time I went home, the last time I funded her bullshit. Then I spend the rest of the weekend being *exactly* like her—drinking myself into oblivion and having sex."

With Veronica.

I knew her name now, though hadn't then.

Hadn't cared to.

Not when I was just looking for oblivion, when I was barely conscious.

"She went to my mom, apparently," I said. "Thought that she could get into contact with me. It didn't take long for her to know that was a dead end. My mom only sucks people dry." I drew in a breath that felt like hot pokers jabbing into my lungs, my next words barely a whisper. "My mom never told me, not when I called to check in on her, not when I slipped up and sent her money a few times after. She just filed it away, stored it to be used against me at the most opportune moment."

Like after becoming national news because of the fire and the game-winning goal for the Cup.

That was a prime blackmail opportunity.

That was the proof that killed the final spark of hope I'd stupidly held on to that she might change, might be different.

Fucked up.

Beyond idiotic.

But I'd officially learned my lesson now.

"What did"—Bailey flipped through the pages—"Veronica say when you talked to her?"

I swallowed, looked away again.

"Axel?" Bailey asked for a moment.

"I—" I clenched my jaw, released it. "I haven't talked to her."

"Then how—" Bailey broke off. "Pascal got this for you."

I nodded.

"I wonder why she didn't reach out to you through the team," Bailey murmured. "When your mom didn't help her."

That was a question I had as well, one that sent a sick feeling swirling through my belly. Had my mother threatened her? Or had she just decided that a fuck-up like me shouldn't be in our son's life? "I don't know."

"So..." My eyes slid back to Bailey's. "What are you going to do?"

That was another question I had.

One that I didn't know the answer to.

How could I move into their lives? How could I disrupt everything they'd built together? How could I insert myself, pretending to be a parent when I'd barely gotten my own life together?

But how could I not?

How could I miss out on any more time with my son?

How could I risk making him think that he wasn't worthy of a father or was unwanted or—any of the other things that *I'd* felt growing up?

I couldn't.

I had to reach out to them, to make contact.

I just...didn't know how.

"We'll figure it out," Bailey murmured, shifting on the bed, coming close, wrapping her arms around me. Her scent filled my nose. Her body pressed to mine, thawing out the ice that had gripped my veins. Then she leaned back enough to cup my cheeks. "Yeah?"

"I don't want him to think—" My voice broke, vision going glassy.

But Bailey didn't hold it against me.

She just held *me*.

"He won't," she whispered.

I rested my forehead on her shoulder, let her hold me, knowing that *this* was what Brit had talked about those weeks ago, knowing that it it if I'd listened to her sooner and just talked to Bailey, the agony that had gripped my insides for these last couple of weeks wouldn't have been there.

But...I was an idiot.

But...luckily the woman who loved me knew that and knew when to push me, knew how not to be pushed *away* from my idiocy.

So, I stayed there, my head on her shoulder, her arms holding me tight, the maelstrom in my gut somewhat soothed. Because of her. Our relationship one that was going to get stronger despite my efforts at going it alone. Because of her. My heart was hers.

Because of who she was inside.

She was the one person on this planet who I could be vulnerable with, the one person who would never hold it against me.

Which was why I vowed that I wouldn't let the same dumb instincts put distance between us.

"You know," she said softly. "I'm usually the one who's a dumbass and doesn't talk things through."

That startled a laugh out of me and I found I could lift my head, that the weight on my shoulders wasn't quite so heavy.

Because of her.

Her thumb brushed over my smile. "You know it's true."

She was the woman who owned me, but she wasn't perfect. She'd been hurt too, and that meant she'd sometimes retreated, sometimes acted without thinking.

Human.

Bailey was human.

And maybe...I guess I was too.

Yes, that sounded stupid, even in my own head, but I was having a revelation here, okay? I was realizing that...I could be an idiot, too, and she would still love me.

So maybe...my son could still love me, even though I hadn't been there.

Hope in my heart, small sparks that grew to something larger.

Because I was going to try.

Bailey's fingers brushed my cheek. "I don't want to wipe this look off your face"—she ran her thumb over my lips again, beneath each eye, as though memorizing my expression—"but I know your mom didn't connect you guys *then*." Her hand dropped to my shoulder, probably because I felt my face harden, knew the look she'd liked had disappeared. She kept talking though, and with one question, the ice was back in my veins.

"How does your mom factor into this now?"

TWENTY-SEVEN

"Moo! *Moo!*"

I grinned at Roxie, who was excitedly petting Picard as Brit held her daughter in her arms, having the distinct thought that this very scenario was likely going to be Picard's future—at least for the foreseeable amount of time.

I'd made it up to Olivia and Cole's ranch.

Visits from kids yelling *Moo!* were sure to be happening on the regular, especially with summer around the corner and Cole's camps fully booked for the next three months.

Picard would love it.

Data would, too.

Though there was still no riding in *my* future, a fact that my horse was definitely not happy about and had made clear to me with her various huffs and puffs when I'd visited her in the pasture. She was a bit too wild for the kids to ride, but Cole had managed to take her out without breaking his neck, so she was getting some exercise at least.

Not that it mattered to Data.

She'd been huffy and standoffish even though she'd been my first stop and I'd brought apples and sugar cubes.

Thankfully, the key to her heart was her stomach, so my oldest baby had forgiven me my absence. Though my oldest baby probably wouldn't forgive me when my youngest baby, Spock, came home with Axel and me. I'd need to buy an apple orchard in order to bribe my way back into her good graces.

Oldest baby. Youngest baby.

All those thoughts of *baby* had me inhaling, knowing that I wouldn't be able to think of that word for a good long while without that noun being tangled up with everything that Axel had told me two nights before.

Yesterday, we'd stayed in bed.

He'd fucked me practically raw—in the best way, if raw could be described as something good. Which it probably couldn't. But anyway, he'd worked his sexual magic and eventually I'd had to cut him off to give us both some time to recover. What I needed was a soak in a long, warm bath, but since that wasn't going to happen with this unwieldy fucking cast, I'd settled for a garbage-bag-wrapped shower and reveling in the fact that I was deliciously sore and every muscle had been turned to jelly, my pussy convulsing at regular intervals, reminding me of how good it had been fucked.

Woe is me.

My life was so hard.

A pussy that was fucked well.

A man who loved me.

Snort.

Anyway, I was still here, still on this planet, which was something that made me feel guilty when I thought about it, when I thought of my neighbors and how their lives had been cut short, but I knew that was survivor's guilt talking, so I was trying to acknowledge the feeling and not shove it down. I was trying to talk about it when I could, to not give it power over me. The guilt was still there, though, and I thought it probably always would.

Was my life complicated? Yes.

With plenty of hurdles and road bumps, especially given the bit of information that Axel had finally shared the night before last? Definitely.

It was also fucking beautiful (with plenty of *fucking*).

Heh.

"Now *that's* a look."

The softly accented voice had me jumping—Pascal, even as I'd gotten to know him a little bit over the last months—was still very, *very* sneaky.

And—not that I could tell based on his placid expression—but I thought that he got a kick out of scaring the shit out of me every time he materialized out of the shadows.

I narrowed my eyes at him, communicating what I thought of his amusement at my expense.

His mouth curved, just slightly.

Something I would have missed if I hadn't been studying him so closely.

But I *was* studying him, wondering about the secrets of this man, knowing I wasn't the person who'd ever get to the heart of them. And still wondering about them anyway.

Ah, well.

The mystery of Pascal would probably never end.

"What look?" I asked instead of pondering that further.

A thumb brushing over my cheek, surprising the shit out of me. His finger was calloused, skin golden, eyes unfathomable. "I'm glad you're okay."

"I—"

"Bay Bay!"

I jumped and turned at Roxie's shrill—albeit adorable—little voice. She was just old enough to start being able to communicate, to put names to faces, but still not old enough to say all of them correctly.

Her name for me might be minus the *-ley,* but I *loved* being

called Bay Bay by the gorgeous little nugget, so it wasn't any skin off my nose.

"Roxie Rox," I called back, glancing back over my shoulder to see that Pascal had fucking disappeared again.

Seriously, I needed to put a bell on him.

"Bay!" More urgent now, so I stopped my search for Pascal, knowing he'd reappear when he wanted to, considering that Axel had asked him to meet us at the ranch so that we could sit down with Olivia and Pascal and come up with a strategy for dealing with Axel's mom.

Who was blackmailing Axel.

Threatening to share something that wasn't bad—no, it wasn't great either. But babies were born every day, and sometimes parenthood was complicated. The fact would ding his public image, and he might lose some sponsorships, especially considering that the offers were coming fast and furious after his game-winning (and game-saving during the previous matchup) play for the Cup. He was fast becoming the face for the Gold, so losing sponsorships would definitely affect his bottom line.

That was the least of his concerns, though Olivia had reminded him that it needed to be one, especially if he wanted to have a plan to take care of his family—which now included a son —in the future.

He'd conceded that point.

But he'd still been more worried about what this bit of news might do to the team and to Cole's ranch, considering that the first sponsorship job he'd taken had been to help fundraise for the programs here.

Far beneath that concern was his need to preserve his income.

And, did I mention that my big, broody hockey player had a huge heart?

Yes.

One that was mine and I was going to do everything to protect.

Which had meant that I'd called in the big guns—Brit and Stefan (who both knew plenty about bad press and how to deal with it), PR Rebecca and her husband and former player for the team, Kevin (both of whom were wicked smart and media savvy), current publicist and Rebecca's protégée, Scarlet and her hubby, and one of the most consistent and popular players on the team, Kayden.

And the biggest risk of all.

I'd sourced the number of Pierre Barie—Stefan's father and the owner of both the Rush and the Gold.

He was en route, and Axel probably wouldn't be happy (especially after he'd snapped at me...and then kissed me breathless when he'd seen the group gathered in the ranch's meeting when we'd first shown up). He didn't get it.

I did.

They did.

Or maybe it was that he just still didn't believe it, believe that his family would have his back.

Well, I was going to *make* him believe it, my stubborn, beautiful, sexy, big, broody hockey player.

And luckily, the rest of the group here was happy to prove it, too.

Pierre had told me he could give us an hour, and I'd jumped at that fact, knowing that an hour with the successful businessman and entrepreneur was worth its weight in gold.

No pun intended.

Heh.

Roxie practically lurched into my arms then and when I scooped her up and held her close and she smoothed her hand over my cheek, patted my smile, grinning back at me, I had to think that Pascal had been right.

My happiness, the happy that was now embedded in my soul, was obvious to the rest of the world.

Maybe once that was something I would have hidden, would have protected.

Now I wanted the rest of the world to know it.

Axel Finnegan was a great man—one who made me deliriously happy.

And he'd still make me happy, even if his mother succeeded in trying to destroy him.

TWENTY-EIGHT

AXEL

I was dying inside.
    Slowly, incrementally dying.
    Or maybe I was being reborn.
    Maybe I was fucking delirious and trying to write shitty ass poetry in my mind that couldn't process all of the people having taken their time out of their vacation or their workday or stepped away from their families.
    For me.
    To help me deal with my fucked-up mother.
    And not *one* of the people in this group, all of whom I respected beyond measure, had looked at me with disapproval or had exchanged thinly veiled insults because of my predicament.
    They'd taken the problem in stride.
    They'd been angry on my behalf.
    And now they were all sitting around this big conference table and thinking of the best way to deal with this.
    Because my mother was...

Well, I'd said it before and I'd say it again.

She was fucked-up.

She was blackmailing me not with the fact that I have a son, but also with the scout story and also with embarrassing information about me, not the least of which was a recording of the final call I'd had with her.

When my head had been messed up from everything I was feeling about Bailey.

It made me sound pathetic, though there wasn't anything truly bad in the recording.

But added to the parade of women I'd fucked, the damage I'd done to the bars and properties in River's Bend, garnering the initial ill-will of the townspeople, the son I hadn't accepted—never mind that I hadn't known about him because of her, but I knew that she was going to spin my absentee parenting to the nth degree.

Which was ridiculous considering she'd gotten the fucking gold medal in shitty parenting.

Still, all of those things together weren't looking good.

Add in the pedestal I was on right now because of hockey and my tracking down Bailey and Olivia was concerned.

Very, very concerned.

It would be very easy to knock me down.

I wasn't perfect—God, I fucking knew that. But I also understood that sometimes people loved nothing more than to tear someone who was on top to shreds.

And, for all intents and purposes, I was on top right now.

A hero who'd found his woman, despite all odds, then had made a stamp on the sports world.

It was something out of a movie.

But it was something that would make the shit my mom wanted to use against me—both truth and fiction—spread like wildfire.

Didn't matter.

I was going to own all of this. I wouldn't lie about my past, and I wouldn't put Veronica through the ringer. She had been through enough.

Alex—my *son*—had, too.

It also didn't pass me by that his name was close to mine (though minus a side of stupid, since Axel was a stupid name for a kid, but Alex was perfectly normal), but I didn't know if it was a coincidence or because Veronica hoped that we might someday connect.

I hoped for the latter.

I braced for the former.

Just like I braced for the shitshow that my mom was going to unleash.

"You guys don't have—" I began after they'd outlined how they were going to handle the fallout.

Brit waved a hand at me, cutting me off in that way she had. It was what had made her a force in the locker room. It was something I was going to miss—not the cutting off, that was annoying, even though I loved her like a sister, but rather it was going to be hard to not have the atmosphere she'd brought to the space.

She'd fostered the guys, me, built us up, left us with ties that were strong as hell.

But I was going to miss *her*.

"We're doing what we have to in order to protect our family," Brit said, eyes drifting to the plate glass window that gave a viewpoint into the play area the next room over.

It was full of Gold kids, another facet of my family.

One that was going to go out and make s'mores and visit the animals some more after we were done with this meeting.

That was the only reason guilt wasn't eating me alive for Bailey having dragged everyone up here.

Olivia and Cole loved hosting people here. The kids had loved visiting the animals and, in particular, had loved mooing at Picard. Spock had been beyond excited to see us, and I hadn't realized how much I'd missed the fuzzball until he'd bounded over, licked my hand, and then permanently stationed himself at Bailey's side.

Helping me look after my woman.

Just like the rest of the mammals in this room.

A thought that almost had me laughing—because I didn't think the perfectly dressed with four-inch heels and a power suit that put Olivia's to shame, Rebecca, would appreciate being referred to as a mere mammal—but I didn't get that far.

Because Rebecca jumped into the conversation. "I didn't get this team—no offense," she added with a glance toward Scarlett, her mini-PR-badass who'd taken over the publicist mantle.

"None taken," Scar said with a smile.

"Good." A no-nonsense nod. "Because I didn't get this team to this place of social media superiority to allow some shitty alcoholic mother to ruin it, to ruin one of *my* players," she said tartly, not holding back. But then again Rebecca *didn't* hold back.

There was a reason the mini-PR-badass Scarlett was doing so well.

Trained at the feet of the master, she was bound to have picked up more than a few tricks.

Pierre nodded—and God, when Pierre *fucking* Barie had walked into the meeting room a half hour before, I'd alternately wanted to throttle the woman I loved and run for the fucking hills.

This was embarrassing.

This was everything I'd worked to overcome.

But...I was finally understanding that this was also family. Okay, maybe I'd already known that and the issue had been that I'd expected the family I'd become a part of to shunt me off. That was what usually happened—or had been my experience in the past. Plus, this wasn't a little problem. This was something that could easily turn toxic.

They'd be within their rights to tell me to fuck right off with my drama.

Except, they weren't.

So maybe I could finally learn to trust in this family we'd built. Trust it wouldn't just be there for the good times.

It would also be there for the fuckups.

All of which meant that I hadn't throttled Bailey.

I clutched her hand, kissed her temple, whispered to her exactly how much her going to bat for me meant.

It was *everything*.

"I agree," Pierre said and I saw the same sort of icy blue steel that Stefan had manifested on the ice when he'd still be playing. This was not someone to be fucked with, business acumen and power aside. Pierre was as determined as one of my teammates— and twice as scary. "No one fucks with my players." He sat back, sighed when he checked his watch, no doubt having somewhere more important to be. But he didn't get up, didn't leave. Instead, he steepled his fingers and said, "But that aside, this needs to be handled with precision."

Nods all around the table. Bailey's fingers clenching around mine.

"So let's all go over the plan for me, step by careful, precise step."

A blip of silence.

And then Rebecca flipped back to the front page of the pad of paper she'd been jotting notes on, Scarlett doing the same beside her.

They exchanged glances, nodded again.

Then Rebecca began to talk.

And as I heard the plan again, this time from start to finish, this time with all the roles everyone needed to play, all the moving parts, all the time and effort that my family was going to put in, I felt my throat get tight.

Thankfully, I didn't need to speak, just had to incline my head in agreement for my part.

But I knew that my family saw what it meant.

And instead of exploiting the weakness...
What I got was support.

Twenty-Nine

Bailey

I was nervous, so nervous that I was having a hard time operating my crutches, so I had no clue as to how Axel appeared so relaxed.

But then again, he'd been relaxed from the moment we'd reached the midpoint of the meeting of minds up at Cole's and Olivia's ranch.

Sanguine.

Comfortable in his own skin.

Even as we were meeting his son.

His. Son.

Rebecca had arranged this—a quiet call to Veronica, an out of the way meeting—and now we were walking (crutching) down the hallway of a luxury hotel several hours south of the city, toward a set of rooms on the top floor.

The presidential suite.

It should be ridiculous to be in a room like that.

But they'd wanted the space to have privacy and this could be framed as a business meeting if word got out before the rest of the plan was unleashed.

They'd factored a lot of variables in, but the single most important one was that Axel's mother wouldn't know the storm was bearing down on her.

I, for one, couldn't wait until those hurricane force winds tore her to shreds.

But, then again, I was protective of my man.

"Slow down, buttercup," he murmured, gripping my arm, holding me steady when the rubberized edge of my crutch threatened to catch on the carpeting.

I hated these crutches.

They were Satan's...Satan's...Satan's dildo, fucking my armpits raw (and that was in a bad raw way, not the delicious Axel way).

But I'd be on them for at least another month.

Freaking cow, steer, fucking middle child of mine for stomping on and breaking the largest bone in my body.

I was lucky, according to the orthopedist, that the fracture hadn't gone all the way through.

That could have killed me.

I told him to add it to the list, behind the flames and smoke inhalation.

He hadn't thought my pithy comment was very funny and neither had Axel. But, alas, I was me and pithy was all I could be.

All of which was to say that I was hardly ever pithy and I'd been damned proud of myself for my quip and...

None of these thoughts were distracting me from the fact that I was about to come face to face with a woman that Axel had made a baby with. A baby she'd named Alex. A baby who she'd made Axel, whose mother had apparently filled her head with such vitriol and nonsense—and maybe threats—that she'd not breathed a word about the child to anyone in Axel's circle.

Not for the entire five years of his existence.

So yeah, I was nervous, really *freaking* nervous.

For a multitude of reasons, not including that fact that we were all of a few minutes away from meeting him and his mother.

"We'll handle it," Axel murmured, not releasing my arm, and making me slow my pace down the hall. Ensuring that I wasn't going to eat shit on the carpet, which *was* luxurious, but also which was something that I didn't want to eat shit on.

That would hurt.

And there were cameras in the hall. Pascal was manning them, making sure the footage didn't leak, but I knew that he'd fucking laugh his ass off if I *did* eat shit.

After making sure I was okay first.

After—

"Relax, buttercup," Axel murmured. "I can practically feel the whirlwind in your mind." He rubbed his temple, smothering a wince, and guilt assuaged me anew. I was making this harder on him, making him comfort me when he needed to focus on the task in front of him.

"Sorry," I whispered.

"Hey," he whispered back, tugging me to a halt and capturing my face between his palms when I would have focused on that plush, albeit ugly, carpeting. "Look at me."

I didn't want to.

But I didn't have any power *not* to.

"*We'll* handle it," he said again, giving my words from a few days before back to me.

They meant...everything and nothing.

Because we were together and *could* handle it. But also, what if it *wasn't* okay? What if he decided that he should be with Veronica—

That thought finally registered in my belly.

And I knew I had to give it to him, knew that was what was prickling my nerves to uncomfortable proportions.

"I'm worried that you'll want to make a family with them," I said, so softly, it barely reached my own ears. "I'm worried that you'll need me to step back and I don't want to stand in the way of—"

His arms wrapped around me so quickly and so tightly that I lost all the air in my lungs.

But he didn't let go, didn't ease up.

Just kept holding me so tightly that it was difficult to breathe.

I was shaking, I realized. From a fear I hadn't truly accepted could take hold but had shoved down because it wasn't the time to think about it when he was telling me what he'd learned, when we were all getting together to solve the mess his mother was laying out on him. But that fear had been there, and it wasn't until it had crossed my mind, my lips that I'd truly understood what I'd buried.

This wasn't the time—*oh* how it wasn't the time.

But Axel didn't get mad at me for dropping this bomb on him.

He just...held me.

And slowly, I managed to breathe, to rest against him, to get that fear to ease enough for my pulse to stop pounding, for my mind to clear.

"I'm sorry," I whispered. "I know this isn't the right—"

"There is no right or wrong between us, buttercup." His palm slid up, cupped my cheek. "There's just you and me and *us*. That won't change, no matter how big our family grows."

Because love wasn't finite. And neither was family.

Brit had shown me that.

So had Billie Rose.

"I know," I whispered.

His face went gentle, and he brushed his lips over mine. Laughing slightly as he pulled away. "It actually makes me feel a little better that you're nervous. You've been holding so much together, superwoman." He tugged a strand of my hair. "I was starting to get a complex."

That startled a laugh out of *me*. "Takes a super person to know one," I teased. "Mr. Crosses Fire Lines to Find His Woman, and oh, no big deal, then becomes Mr. Scores the Game-Winning Goal."

He snorted. "You would have found your way out without me. I just...sped up the process."

Maybe.

But also, probably not.

Thankfully, that wasn't something we needed to focus on right then.

Not when we were five feet away from a door that, when opened, was going to forever change the course of our lives.

Eeek.

That was terrifying to think about.

Another tug of my hair. "Breathe."

"You and your commands," I muttered.

"You like it when I give you commands."

"In bed," I countered.

A wicked smile that was so hot, so tempting, so much like *my* Axel that it took my breath away. "Yeah." A nip to my bottom lip. "So, I'll give you some tonight."

I shouldn't be turned on in this instance.

I still was.

But I found that I didn't care, *couldn't* care.

Not with Axel by my side.

"Ready?" he asked.

I nodded, took my hand off my crutch for a brief moment to give him a two-fingered salute. "Yes, sir."

Another nip on my bottom lip, this one turning into a full-blown kiss—one that left me breathless and wondering if I should just accept the inevitable and lower myself onto the plush, ugly carpet beneath my feet and spread my legs for him. "More of that later tonight," he murmured.

"The yes sir?" I asked. "Or the fingering?"

He'd started to move past me, hand lifting to knock.

My questions had him choking on air, surprised eyes hitting mine.

I waggled my brows.

And he gave me the most wonderful thing ever.

His laughter.

It was warm and robust and filled my heart and soul and ears...

Just as the door he'd been about to knock on swung open.

THIRTY

AXEL

I expected to feel something different.

To feel *something*.

But all I had was an odd sort of numbness when I looked at the woman who'd given birth to a kid who belonged to me—or at least to a kid who possessed half of my DNA.

Veronica's eyes gentled when she looked at me, and then she stepped back and into the room, holding the door wide as I allowed Bailey to go in ahead of me. I caught the heavy panel when she released it once Bailey was clear, letting it close without slamming.

Then I flicked the lock.

I'd spent enough time in hotel rooms to make that instinct.

My gaze moved around the room, searching for Alex and not finding him, even as disappointment grew in my belly. He wasn't here. She'd decided not to bring him. Which I got, considering that my mother had turned her away, had painted me in the same broad strokes of someone who wouldn't look after her, wouldn't look after Alex.

But...I was disappointed.

Something Bailey must have sensed because she paused next to me, shifting so her shoulder brushed mine.

Telling me she was there, would be there, no matter the outcome.

"He's in the bedroom."

Blinking, I glanced away from the empty couch, that dismay slipping into confusion as I looked back at Veronica.

"Alex is having some quiet time," she whispered. "It was a bit of a drive."

My throat worked.

"Sorry about the drive," Bailey murmured. "I'm sure it's not easy to travel with a young kiddo, especially that far."

Veronica smiled and I remembered her now. Remembered why I'd been drawn to her, the drunken haze fading just enough for me to recall the quiet brunette, nursing a glass of wine and reading on her phone. Pretty, but extremely shy. I'd taken it as a challenge to get her to loosen up.

And had left her raising a kid on her own for the last five years.

Cool.

Go me.

"Did you guys want to sit down?" She inclined her head to the couch, gentle and soft and warm.

She should be pissed at me.

Why wasn't she pissed at me?

Thankfully, Bailey was much less of a statue than I was. She nodded and moved across the room so she could take a seat on the couch, asking Veronica about the drive up from the LA area as she went.

That was where my mom lived now, had lived ever since I'd gone pro.

In a house she'd bought with *my* money.

Rage churned through me and I wanted to pick up the coffee table, to launch it at the plate glass window. But I was also aware that rage was a useless emotion right now. There was nothing that I could do to change what had happened and coffee-table-launching wasn't the most dad-like thing to be doing.

It would probably send Veronica packing, and then I'd miss out on—

"I heard about the fire," Veronica said softly. "Did you lose your house?"

Bailey inhaled softly, pain etched into her face. "Unfortunately, yes."

"I'm so sorry," she said, reaching over and squeezing Bailey's hand. "I—can you rebuild?"

Another inhale. "I have insurance," Bailey said softly. "But I'm not sure I can rebuild all that was lost. It was a family property," she added when Veronica's brows pulled together. "A lot of the outbuildings and fencing were lost, along with our house. The history—" A shake of her head. "I know I'll rebuild something, but I'm not sure what form it'll be."

"Too soon to make those decisions." It was a statement, but also kind of a question.

Bailey nodded in answer.

Silence fell, the soft chitchat dissolving and both Veronica and Bailey looking at their hands, probably searching for something to say, considering I wasn't contributing, that I was standing there like a big, dumb rock and—

"What does he for quiet time?" I blurted.

Not gently.

Not quietly.

I'd like to think it was warmly, but I wasn't sure it was that either, not when the volume was wrong and—

"He likes to watch a movie on the iPad." Her gaze flicked to mine and then away. "He doesn't get electronics for hours and hours a day, I promise. Just a bit on days like this when we both need a break."

"We all need a break sometimes," Bailey said into the silence that fell again, uncomfortable and taut and—

I stopped thinking of all the things that I was desperate to know about Alex, about all of the explanations that I owed Veronica. That was getting me nowhere except stuck in the fucked-up place that was my head and it wasn't helping anyone.

Level with her.

Right.

I moved to the coffee table, and sat on it, facing both women.

Bailey's leg shifted, pressing to mine, silent, steady support for me as I looked Veronica straight in the eye and said, "I'm sorry."

Veronica's gaze dropped to her hands, but not before her eyes went a little misty. "I-it's okay. We were young and—"

I reached forward, took her hands. "I'm sorry," I said again. "My mother...she didn't tell me that you—"

"I know."

That had me straightening in surprise.

Her head popped up. "Or I know *now*. I...I was young and hurt and you..." A breath. "You'd made me feel special. So when your mom told me I was just like dozens of other girls, that I'd never get close to you again...I was hurt."

"Veronica—"

Her throat worked again, but her chin came up. "I was stupid, too. I thought I'd go to your house, that you'd tell me it would all be okay and we'd get married and..." A shake of her head. "I thought that you were my ticket out of my stupid, boring life. Your mom made it clear that she wouldn't let it happen and...I hadn't found my spine yet." Her eyes flicked to the closed bedroom door. "I hadn't found it for him yet. I should have talked to *you*, should have done anything except what I did, which was move away from town and claw out an existence for us on my own. I could have given him so much more, could have been a better mother, worked less—"

She shook her head, that silence falling again.

I squeezed her hands. "I should have been there for you. I—"

"So when Rebecca called and wanted to arrange this meeting," she said over me, as though the explanation had begun to come and she couldn't stop it, not now. "I pressed her to answer some questions before I agreed to this. Because I was absolutely furious that you'd reach out *now*." A shaky breath. "I don't need you now. I *needed* you then."

I flinched.

Bailey reached out and grabbed my knee, holding me steady when I might have gotten up, might have paced away.

Might have missed the rest of what Veronica was saying.

"But then Rebecca explained that you'd just found out about Alex." Veronica pressed her lips together, was quiet for several more moments, searching, carefully putting the words together, her tone almost gentle when she said, "And I realized that you might actually have been the man I'd glimpsed that night."

"I wasn't," I told her quickly.

She sat back slightly, tugged on her hands.

I didn't release them, couldn't until she understood. "I wasn't that man, wasn't the man to step up and be father of the year. I was..." I sighed. "I wasn't in the right frame of mind to be the man you both needed, even if I *want* to think that I would have stepped up for you both once I'd found out about the pregnancy, would have been there for you every moment." I cleared my throat, my tone more than a little raspy with emotion. "The truth is that I was fucked up for a long time—" My eyes flicked to Bailey's, held for a few heartbeats, before I managed to press on. "Even now I...I'm not sure I can be what he needs, what you need." A breath, hope welling in my heart. "But I at least would like to be able to try."

"Not exactly a ringing endorsement of yourself," Veronica said, her tone cool.

I nodded, released a breath. "I won't lie to you. Not after all I've missed."

Her lips pressed flat again, but this time it was almost as if she was trying to smother a deep-seated and heavy emotion.

Considering I was doing the same, I didn't comment on it.

I just held her hands, her gaze, willing her to understand, hoping that we might find some way out of this. "I don't want him to grow up like I did," I told her. "I don't want him to think his dad didn't want him, to be desperate and searching for approval in other places, hurting when he doesn't find it. I don't want him to have this *hole*"—I released one hand, slammed it to my chest, beneath which, my heart was pounding—"inside him that can never be filled because he's always thinking that the reason I wasn't there was because he wasn't good enough."

Bailey released a shuddering breath, her fingers clamped to my thigh, and I realized that she was crying, silent tears leaking out of the corners of her lashes.

Veronica, too, was emotional, her eyes damp, her throat bobbing.

"He deserves to be loved, and I promise you that I will do my best to make sure that he *never* feels the lack of me, of my absence, not ever again."

Silence.

Long and fraught with tension.

And Veronica not looking at me.

THIRTY-ONE

BAILEY

I willed Veronica to accept Axel's explanation, to be as moved by it as I was.

I knew how much it cost him to say what he'd just said, to admit what he'd admitted, to expose the wounds he carried deep inside.

But Veronica didn't reply.

Just sat there next to me in a silence that grew increasingly more tense.

Until I was about to burst out of my skin and throttle her until she understood.

Violent, yes. But also...she *had* to understand.

I kept my hand on Axel's thigh, the other gripping the handle of one of my crutches, tightening as the silence went on.

"Fuck," Veronica said.

I blinked, gaze jerking up to her face.

She turned her hands over in Axel's, shifting so that she was holding him instead of the other way around.

"Fuck," she said again, a barely audible whisper. "I want to be mad at you. I *want* to hate you."

My lungs inflated so quickly that my mostly healed ribs ached. "But..."

Axel's expression killed me.

"But I know something of what it's like to have a mother whose sole purpose it is to fuck with your life, with your head, with your heart."

I exhaled.

"So," she said softly. "I'm sorry I went away, sorry that I didn't find you after your mom threatened me. I'm sorry that I didn't find my spine until recently." She swallowed and her chin came up. "I'll accept your apology for not being here, and we'll both be mad at the proper people—your mother for acting like she did, mine for breaking me down so completely, I couldn't see past my own face."

"Just that easy?" Axel asked.

Veronica's mouth turned up. "I have the feeling that none of this will be easy. But I'm going to try." A blip of quiet. "Just like I know you are as well. And together"—now she looked at me too, and I nodded, wanting her to know that I was right there with her on the fucked-up parents and also with the this-being-something-we-would-do-together part—"we'll make Alex know that he's always loved, always wanted, always a part of a family that will look out for him."

"Yes," I said softly. "You're part of us now. You're not alone."

Maybe I shouldn't have stepped in, shouldn't have spoken in this scenario that was far from being centered around me.

But I needed Veronica to know that I was with her.

That Alex was innocent and had a place in our lives, in *my* life.

I wouldn't ever make him feel unwanted, not after having been subjected to a lifetime of that very same thing.

"Thank you," she whispered, releasing one of Axel's hands and gripping my own. "I know this was probably not in your plan."

My lips turned up. "Neither was having a big, broody, hockey player for a boyfriend," I said, trying to lighten the mood. "But I dealt with him and all *that*"—a smile in his direction—"I can definitely get along with you, with Alex. Because you matter. *Both* of you," I added softly, seeing that emotion tear through her expression again. "You're family and soon you'll see that with us, with the Gold that means there's no getting out. You're stuck with us. Pucks in, no outs."

Veronica's laughter was a bit watery, but her voice was steady when she said, "We've been alone for a while. Getting stuck with you guys sounds just about perfect."

Great, now my smile was watery. "Good."

Axel squeezed her hand then covered the back of mine where it was still resting on his leg.

The silence fell, but only for a few moments this time, because then they were discussing all the things that Alex liked—all of which were things that I was becoming intimately family with thanks to the gaggle of Gold kiddos. Minecraft. Legos. The occasional graphic novel. Watching people play video games on YouTube. Watching people unbox things on YouTube. Watching...YouTube. He was also into horses (win for me) and was currently watching *Black Beauty*.

I told her about Data and Picard and Spock (and their hand in saving me from the fire, which she demanded that I tell Alex, because he would *die*—her words, not mine).

She shared that they'd watched some Gold hockey and that he knew he was going to meet someone today, but that he didn't know it was his dad.

"I didn't want to get his hopes up," she murmured. "Just in case things didn't"—her teeth found her bottom lip for a beat before she released it—"go well between us."

"I understand," Axel murmured.

And I knew he did, knew that Veronica realized that as well when he asked a bunch of other questions—favorite color and food (blue and cheese pizza), what sports he liked to play (soccer and baseball), if he liked certain music or songs (anything pop-related because that was all Veronica listened to), if they'd gone on vacation at all and what was their favorite (Disney and the Grand Canyon).

"Though only for about two minutes," Veronica said, her eyes bright with her memories. "Then he was like, *Is this it?* And *I* was like, *Is this it?* And that *was* it. Just a giant hole in the ground...so we ended up going back to my car, turning on the audiobook of *The Lion, The Witch, and The Wardrobe* and drove to the Petrified Forest. He liked that much better." Her lips turned up. "He pretended to be a dinosaur all day so he'd be as old as the trees."

I laughed. "Sounds like he's smart."

"*So* smart."

Axel's fingers squeezed mine. "Must have gotten that from his mom," he said softly.

Veronica inhaled, opened her mouth to reply.

But then the bedroom door opened and a tiny head poked out. "Mom?"

Between one instant and the next, my stomach tied itself into knots, and I knew Axel felt the same when his hand tightened convulsively around mine, hard enough that a bolt of pain shot up my arm. But I barely felt it because then Veronica said, "Come here, honey."

A moment of hesitation.

Then the door opened farther.

And Alex walked out, headphones still covering his ears, the cord dangling at his side and plugged into the tablet he carried. "Yeah, Mom?"

"I want you to meet Axel and Bailey."

Axel was a statue again.

And I was no better.

But then Alex was rounding the table, moving to sit by his mom on the couch, curling into her lap. "Hi," he said shyly.

Veronica wrapped her arms around her son and I watched her shoulders rise and fall on a deep, slow breath. "Axel is your dad, honey."

I braced.

Hell, I wasn't sure I even breathed.

I knew that Axel didn't as we waited to see what Alex would say, how he would respond. Would there be tears? Questions? Anger?

How would a five-year-old react to meeting his father for the first time?

In the end, it wasn't in any way that I would have ever predicted.

Alex glanced from his mom to Axel to me, was quiet for a couple of seconds. Then he shrugged, said, "Okay," and asked Veronica if it was time for dinner.

I shot my gaze to Axel's, worried that he'd be disappointed in the response, but his expression was filled with so much love that I immediately wanted to throw away my birth control and have a dozen babies with him.

He had *so* much love to give.

"Would it be okay if we all eat together?" he asked softly.

Alex turned back to Axel, tilted his head to the side, studying his father closely. "What are we going to eat?"

Luckily, we'd been primed with key intel, and Axel used the insider knowledge to say, "Pizza?"

A bit of suspicion drawing Alex's brows together. "What kind?"

"Cheese," Axel said. "Because that's the best kind, of course."

Alex's brows relaxed and then he nodded sagely. "It is the best."

Veronica squeezed him gently. "What do you say, honey? Should we eat with Axel and Bailey?"

A tilt of his head, consider. "Okay," he declared a moment later, sounding like the most regal of kings. "We can eat together."

I smothered a laugh, saw Veronica do the same.

And I knew that things wouldn't be perfect, but they'd be okay.

Because we'd figure it out together.

And because I was always going to have a cheese pizza on speed dial.

Thirty-Two

Axel

"What does a dad do?" Alex asked the following day.

We'd eaten pizza, had watched *Black Beauty* from start to finish (and I'd gotten to see Bailey sniff away tears because my horse crazy woman loved the movie and especially the ending). But then Alex had been getting a little cranky—not a surprise after the long drive and having to meet two strange people, one of whom was his dad.

So, Bailey and I had gone back down the hall, to the room that Rebecca had reserved for us.

We'd made it *maybe* another thirty minutes before we'd both passed out and slept all the way until about an hour before.

Then we'd showered, met Veronica and Alex for breakfast (and I'd learned that pancakes were also one of his favorite foods).

Now we were at the park.

And Alex and I were making quick work of this jungle gym.

Who knew I could still climb like I was five years old?

I sat down on one side of the double slide, giving myself time to come up with an answer to his question as he clambered down next to me.

"What do you want your dad to do?" I asked, stalling.

I didn't know what a dad did.

I hadn't had one.

I...wasn't sure I knew how to be one.

I was going to damned well try, but...questions like this threw me.

Alex didn't immediately answer me, but I was learning he wasn't the kind of kid to rush into anything. He was calm and thoughtful, as was his reply when it came a few moments later. "Play with me," he said, pushing off and shooting down the slide.

Chuckling, I followed him, legs creaking a bit as I found my feet, because the slides were set low to the ground, *way* low, and I was tall, so not landing on my ass in the tanbark meant that I had to do some quick maneuvering. Alex didn't rush off until I'd stood up, but once I'd made it up, he led the way to a green pole that led to the second story of the play structure, though luckily, this one was surrounded in a spiraling outer pole that I could climb.

"And eat pizza with me," Alex said as he made his way up. "And pancakes," he added once I began to follow him.

"So we've got that part covered," I said, climbing after him, making sure he was steady, that he wouldn't fall.

A nod as he stretched a foot out, spanning the distance and making me hold my breath.

He made it onto the black platform.

I relaxed, focused on my own climb.

"What else?" I asked.

Brows furrowing, he considered my question.

"He would come to my soccer games."

"I can do that."

"And watch YouTube with me."

I nodded. "That, too."

But now he paused, teeth worrying his bottom lip, eyes drifting away. "Live with Mom and me."

I nearly ate shit off that twisting pole, but luckily, I managed to snag the handhold and pull myself onto the platform next to him. "I live with Bailey, bud. Because she and I love each other."

A pause. "And you and Mom don't?"

"We love *you*."

A frown between his brows. "Oh."

"Your mom and I are friends"—they were starting to become them, anyway, and I was determined to make that the truth—"and Bailey and your mom are friends," I added. "So that makes it really cool for you. You have three adults who love you."

Quiet.

So quiet for long enough that my insides churned.

"Like Cassie."

I blinked, not understanding the reference. "Is she a YouTuber?" I asked, having already had my lack of knowledge of popular YouTubers exposed several times that morning.

Alex laughed. Hard. "No, Dad." More laughter. "She's my friend at school."

I was still recovering from the fact that he'd called me *Dad*, so it took me a minute to process the second half of his statement. "Cassie has three people who love her?"

Sweet Jesus, don't let this be me opening up a discussion about a thruple.

"Four," Alex said, matter of factly, shaking his head, and for a moment, I was distracted, thinking I'd seen someone watching us from between the shadows in the distance. But when I glanced back toward the trunks, there was no one there.

Weird.

I shrugged.

It was probably another parent watching over their kiddo. Either that or I was slightly delirious. Alex was awesome, but exhausting.

"Four?" I asked, refocusing on my son.

"Yup." A jerky nod. "Her mom and dad divorced and they both got another person they married, too, so Cassie has two moms and two dads."

"Oh, that's cool," I said, relieved to not have corrupted my child during our first serious conversation.

"Yup." The p at the end popped before he started for the slides again. "I thought of something else dads do," he said as he plunked down on the molded plastic.

"What's that?" I asked, sitting down next to him.

"They give great hugs."

Aw, fuck.

This kid was going to be the death of me.

"How do I rate on the hug scale?" I asked.

A shrug. "Fine," he said with brutal *kid* honesty, "but I know you'll get better with practice."

Truer words, I knew, had never been spoken.

———

"We'll be down next week," I said softly, not wanting to wake Alex, who'd passed out in the back seat.

They'd had breakfast and playground time. Lunch and spending some time hiking in the forest. Then they'd grabbed dinner—not cheese pizza this time, but it *was* mac n cheese, so his son had been satisfied.

On the way back to the hotel, the busy day had caught up with Alex and he'd fallen asleep, slumped back against the headrest of his booster seat.

Bailey had waited with a sleeping Alex while he and Veronica went back up to the room, the latter making quick work of packing up and checking to be sure they hadn't left anything behind since she'd decided to take advantage of Alex's sleeping and start the drive down to SoCal that evening.

I didn't like the idea of her on the road through the night, but I got it.

They'd both sleep better in their own beds.

And if they left now, it would be just a bit after one in the morning by the time they made it.

"He'll be excited," she said, zipping the top of her purse.

"And I'll practice my Dad Hugs," I said lightly. "Since I clearly need more practice."

"I'd die of embarrassment," she said with a smile before bending to check under the bed and finding a small stuffed toy. "Except, one of my favorite things about my boy is that I always know where I stand with him."

I grinned, leaning back against the wall, gaze dropping to their suitcase, packed and ready at my feet, waiting as she ran through her mental checklist.

"Though"—the sudden seriousness of her tone had me looking up, studying her face—"I can't really say that he's *my* boy anymore, can I?"

"What?"

"He's ours." A shaky breath that had me pushing off the wall. "Ignore me," she whispered, pushing back her hair. "I'm just...it's been an emotional few days."

Because I'd come in and imploded it. Again.

I moved to her, tugging her into my arms, knowing Bailey wouldn't begrudge me giving Veronica the hug she so clearly needed. There was something soft and vulnerable about Veronica that called to the protective streak he'd buried, called to the same one that Bailey had in her.

Three people brought together via childhood trauma.

Cool.

But it was also three people who'd been brought together by a little boy who already owned a chunk of my heart.

I smoothed my hand down her hair. "It's okay to be

emotional. I was...well, I still am a bit of a wreck. I just...part of me is always surprised when my mom does something to fuck me over. I know I shouldn't be. I just..." I sighed.

"Expect things to be different," Veronica finished.

"Yeah," I agreed. "But more than that, I hate that she affected you and Alex. I—you guys—we all—" My throat got tight. "I'm just really sorry that you had to do it on your own for the last five years." I released her, crouched a little to meet her eyes, hating that they were damp. "I promise that you both won't be alone again."

Her exhale was shaky, her smile equally brittle, but she squeezed my shoulder and gave me honestly. "It'll take me time to trust in that."

I knew that.

I understood it.

I still fucking hated it.

"We'll be down next week."

Her hand dropped to her side, fingers clenching into a fist, but she nodded. "Okay."

It would take time to build a friendship with this woman who'd been hurt because of me, time and practice to be the father that Alex deserved.

Once I wouldn't have believed I could get there.

Now...I knew differently. I *knew* I would.

So, I just nodded, grabbed their suitcase, and led Veronica to the door, the elevator, the car. "Things might get a little hot for a while once Rebecca starts with everything," I said as we walked.

Everything being the plan we'd come up with at Cole and Olivia's place.

To own my past.

To make sure my mother never interfered in my life again.

"I know," Veronica said softly, holding the car door steady as Bailey used it to haul herself out of the seat. *Haul* because my stubborn, independent woman wouldn't accept any help when she could do it herself—of course, she wouldn't. Once she was steady on her feet, Veronica passed Bailey her crutches. "Rebecca told me the plan and gave me her number." V glanced between Bailey and I. "I have both of yours, too. I'll call you if there are any issues."

Quiet words. Quiet with a dash of forlorn and I wanted to say something that would make this all okay.

But no words would do that.

It would just take...*time*.

Yeah, I was really going to hate that word.

Bailey's fingers brushed mine and I leaned closer, wrapping an arm around her shoulders, telling myself I was steadying her when really, she'd been *my* steady in this.

Veronica smiled, but it was laced with more than a bit of pain and regret. "Next week," she said.

I nodded.

Bailey reached forward and squeezed her hand, suddenly earnest when she said, "I can stay up here." A glance up at me. "Give you guys some family time."

That pain and regret erased themselves from Veronica's face in an instant and she moved close to Bailey before I could get between them, her expression thunderous. "Don't you *ever* say that." She clasped Bailey's cheeks in her palms. "Not *ever*. Alex needs more people in his life who love him, and I know that you'll be one of them. So, that makes us family in every way that matters." Her hands shook slightly. "*Every* way."

"Okay," Bailey whispered.

"I'm sad because I was an idiot who made my baby miss out on this, on *both* of you." A flick of her gaze to mine, telling me that was the truth, but also that there might be something else there, something buried I wasn't yet privy to.

Time.

Yup. Fucking hated that word.

Slender arms wrapping around Bailey's shoulders, a hug that

lasted longer than it probably should, considering that these two women had just met.

When they both pulled back, it was with damp eyes.

And I knew that, yeah, it was going to take time to get fully there.

But I also knew that we *would* get there.

That the family we were building was going to kick ass.

THIRTY-THREE

BAILEY

There were reporters outside our apartment.

Well, not in the hall, but they were on the street, several stories below, the late afternoon sunlight glinting off camera lenses when I dared to move the curtain a fraction of an inch to peek out.

A gaggle of middle-aged men in dumpy clothes who could yell my name in a way that sent a chill down my spine.

I didn't like it.

I liked it even less that I still had a week to go on my crutches and that I wasn't fast enough on them to get away from the photographers whose cameras made loud whirring and clicking sounds when they shot a million frames per second or the reporters who loved to shove microphones or cell phones with their recording apps on and at the ready under my nose. The reporters, both male and female, were better dressed than the paparazzi and cameramen, but they were equally annoying.

I'd known what I was getting into, though.

Rebecca and Scarlett had made every step of the plan we were implementing very clear.

And, truthfully, it had all been okay.

There'd been a bit of a kerfuffle when the story first broke, but Axel had settled that with a nationally aired interview and several videos on TikTok. He'd given his side of the story, and though not all of the press coming at him had been positive, it had been manageable, and most of the people he'd interacted with or who'd been commenting on his videos had appreciated the honest way he'd owned his shit.

It had helped that the media had then gotten pictures of him having a tea party with Alex and his best friend from school, Cassie. The little girl was adorable, but then again, so were Alex *and* Axel, especially when he'd dutifully worn the tiara Cassie had plunked on his head while he'd sipped from a tiny mug that was absolutely dwarfed in his big, broad hand.

The photographs had been a violation, taken by a neighbor over the fence between Veronica's back yard and their own.

But they'd also shown the softer side of Axel.

And Alex, for that matter, whose favorite activities skewed fairly far away from tea parties and tiaras.

He and Axel had indulged Cassie, though.

The photos had indulged the public.

But what had really turned the tide was Billie Rose and the others taking his back. River's Bend had been in the news plenty, what with the city attorney filing a lawsuit against several insurance companies who were trying to screw over its residents, even though they had fire insurance and had paid their premiums, because evidence had been brought to light that the cause of the fire had been arson.

Arson.

A person had been responsible for starting the flames.

That was...unfathomable and infuriating and—

It made me sad.

People had died. Others had lost everything.

Because some idiot—who hadn't been caught yet—had been playing with matches.

And then the insurance companies weren't even going to follow through on their expectations?

Yeah, that wasn't a good look for the well-to-do and profit-hungry companies, so it was no surprise that public opinion was highly negative on that fact. However, I knew from personal experience that Billie was a dog to the bone. She'd made certain that River's Bend had stayed relevant as the paperwork was filed and was still keeping the town in the headlines as the rebuilding slowly got underway. I thought it was highly likely the companies would pay out or settle the suit and that residents would get their money.

My aunt was a badass.

Meanwhile, I was stuck hobbling around on crutches by day and packing supply kits by night, adding in the occasional visit up to River's Bend and down to Alex when Axel could take me to either place.

Axel, too, had been busy.

With the interview requests and several commercials and ad campaigns. With Alex and his soccer games and building a slow but strong bond with his son. And with River's Bend. He'd spent a lot of time helping Joel and Ryan and the rest of his former teammates get settled in their temporary housing.

The Rush had lost everything too.

The rink. Their homes. Their equipment.

While Axel had helped with the move, I'd been stuck at City Hall, one of the few buildings downtown that had been spared the flames, and had coordinated.

No surprise, it wasn't my favorite activity.

I preferred to be out there, getting my hands dirty, not looking at Excel spreadsheets and making phone calls to beg for supplies.

But I'd done it.

Because the people of River's Bend were my family just as much as the Gold were.

They needed help, and because of my infernal cast and slowly healing body, that was the only way I could assist.

So, I had.

Photographs of Axel working out there—lucky man, getting *his* hands dirty—had also been front and center of many a news story. And that final image, of a man helping out former teammates, working hand in hand with the people who supposedly hated him (if those spinning the tales of his destructive attitude in the media could be believed) had been the final piece of the puzzle.

Then the stories had been less about Axel and women getting their fifteen minutes of fame by sharing stories of his drunken antics, and more about his mother and how awful she'd been in that role.

Old coaches had come forward and shared how she'd sexually assaulted them. Old teammates had given very similar—and uncomfortable—stories.

A former teacher had recalled a time she'd come to a parent-teacher conference drunk, needing to have the cops called on her so that she didn't force Axel into the car with her.

An ex-girlfriend from high school had pulled up old Facebook messages that showed the vitriol that his mother had launched at her for "daring to take her son away."

Her neighbors related the nightmare of living next door to Clarice Finnegan, even as some intrepid reporter discovered that Axel had paid for her house.

All of which had been all part of Rebecca and Scarlett's plan.

Discrediting the trash that was Axel's mom, making the public despise her as much as I did, as we all did. Luckily, *that* hadn't been hard, just like it hadn't been hard, either, to meet Axel's only demand: that they not lie.

Lying hadn't been necessary.

Clarice had spent a lifetime making enemies.

Now they were coming out of the woodwork like it was termite swarming season.

But her regular appearance on the gossip sites and on TikTok as people shared more and more instances of her assholeness weren't the reasons why the paparazzi were on the street out front of the apartment building.

Nope.

That came from the news today.

Something we *hadn't* predicted. Something that hadn't been part of Rebecca's and Scarlett's plan. I supposed none of us were dastardly enough to have thought of it—or maybe, we hadn't believed it would actually happen.

But it had.

Clarice Finnegan had been arrested today and had been taken on a very public perp walk from her front door to the police car and then from that car into the station, media crowded all around on both instances.

And the charges had been released or ferreted out.

Sexual assault.

Extortion.

Drunk and disorderly.

Trespassing.

I wasn't sure if any—or all—would stick, but, man, had it been *satisfying* to see her led out in handcuffs on national television.

I hadn't met the woman—and hopefully would never have to —but it had still brought a smile to my face.

The only unfortunate part?

Because we hadn't known about the charges, hadn't know the arrest was coming, we weren't prepared.

Alex and Axel were out and presumably didn't know that Clarice had been hauled off in handcuffs. They'd gone to Pier 39 and the Exploratorium, hitting the touristy sights even though there was a risk of being stopped with everything that had hit the media. But this was Alex's first visit to the city, so Axel had wanted to do it right.

And things had been relatively calm before the news broke.

Now, though, I was feeling more than a little on edge.

I wasn't alone.

Veronica, having decided to let Axel have time alone with Alex, was curled up on the couch, a glass of wine in her hand, her book forgotten in lieu of the television. We'd planned on some girl time, something I knew was a rarity for her because she'd been doing the heavy lifting when it came to parenting, but the news about Axel's mother had derailed that.

She'd grown increasingly more tense as the minutes went by, as the news continued to play in the background.

And now V wasn't the picture of glee or relaxation.

She was the visage of nerves.

"Right," I said, knowing that it was time to shut off the TV and focus on something else. "Let's—"

She spun toward me, eyes wide, panic clear as day on her face. "Do you think my baby will be all right?"

"Of course he will," I said, frowning. "Axel will—"

"But what if those men who're outside surround them and he gets scared?" She bit her lip. "He's not used to being without me and—"

"I texted, Axel," I said gently. "When I saw the news, I gave him a heads up. I'm sure they're both—"

She jumped up.

Spock, who'd been sitting next to her, followed suit, whining softly.

And, yeah, gentle wasn't penetrating in the least bit.

Now she was heading for the shoe rack, yanking down the gray sneakers she'd set there a couple of hours before.

"V—"

"I need to get to my baby. I need to get to him *right now*."

Mind prickling because this reaction wasn't the Veronica I knew (though, in fairness, I didn't know her all that well since it had only been a couple of weeks), I debated what to do.

But then that debate ended.

Because Veronica reached for the door and yanked it open.

Thirty-Four

Axel

My phone buzzed with another text, drawing my focus from where I'd been staring into the crowd, thinking I'd caught a glimpse of a distinctive blond I hadn't seen in months, and back to my son. I'd been messaged often enough over the last couple of hours to make me want to launch the damned thing over the railing, so I didn't give it more than a cursory look before shoving it back into my pocket.

No one was dying or in the hospital. Nothing was on fire.

Bailey had texted an hour before, telling me everything was fine.

That was reassurance enough. Everyone else could wait.

I was with my son.

I wanted this time.

Uninterrupted.

But I checked it because Bailey was at home and she was still healing. Not to mention she and Veronica were alone, having some girl time, and while Bailey hadn't given *any* indication that she was uncomfortable spending time with my baby mama—had, in fact, made a huge effort to include Veronica in *everything*—I couldn't help but worry that the shine was going to wear off that relationship at some point.

Bailey was mine.

Veronica wasn't. Hadn't ever been.

But did some small part of her think things might change now that I was back in their lives? Was some small part of *me* wondering if she'd tried to sabotage my relationship?

Possibly.

Was I fully aware this made me a cocky asshole?

Yes.

Didn't mean I stopped worrying, though. Didn't mean I stopped looking for any sign that things weren't okay in paradise.

Didn't mean—

"Look, Dad!"

Fuck, my kid undid me when he called me that. I...hadn't thought I'd get there with him. Not this soon. But he had the same gentle, sweet nature that Veronica did.

Not a surprise, I supposed, shoving my phone back in my pocket.

She'd been the only parent in his life.

Biting back the guilt, the regret in missing out on so much, I focused on my son who was currently strapped to some heavy-duty elastic thing with a trampoline below him and a leather belt around his little hips. He was jumping, the elastic bringing him higher than he normally would have been able to leap, and when my gaze came back to his, he shouted again, "Look!"

And then he did a back flip.

He was strapped in. He couldn't fall and the bouncy trampoline and stretchy ropes clearly gave him the ability to complete the flip.

I was still beyond fucking proud to see him do that.

Kind. Empathetic. Open.

And just a dash of daredevil.

He was an easy kid to love.

"Nice, bud!" I called, knowing my smile was huge and probably a bit dopey. But I had a kid and he called me *Dad* and did backflips while strapped into stretchy things. Life was pretty fucking great. Especially, with Bailey in it, with Veronica in it, with Billie Rose and Brit and the guys. Even better now that the media attention had died down (today aside, because I'd noticed more than a few cell phones surreptitiously taking photos in the last hour, no doubt fueled by the fact that we were in tourist-heavy areas).

My life was good.

I was happy.

The people who mattered to me were happy, too.

My cell buzzed again, and since it was just a text from Brit, I slid it back into my pocket. I was going to have a shit-ton of messages to return tonight, but right now was just Alex and Axel time, and yes, I was referring to myself in third person, and no, I didn't care.

But then my cell vibrated. *Again.*

"Christ," I muttered, yanking it out, seeing that Bailey was calling. My annoyance faded, even though I still wasn't pleased at the interruption. "Hey, buttercup."

"We have a situation," she said quietly.

"What's that noise in the background?" I said, my stomach immediately clenching.

"I need you to switch to FaceTime and I need you to put the camera on Alex. Can you do that?"

"I—why?"

"Axel."

Warning in her voice had me stifling the rest of my questions. I pulled the phone from my ear, pointed it at Alex who was still bouncing on the trampoline, the elastic bands pulling him higher, and hit the button to turn it into a video call.

Veronica's face immediately came on the screen, panic written in her eyes in a way that I hadn't seen before.

"Where is—" She cut herself off, face gentling as she presumably saw Alex bouncing.

Her relieved breath was loud through the speakers.

"Dad, look!" Alex called again. And then he did another back flip.

Veronica gasped, and I watched in complete and total confusion as she started crying. Big tears leaking out of the corners of her eyes, her skin pale, her hand shaking as she lifted it, pressed it to her mouth.

Then I was watching her sink down to the ground, her forehead pressed to her knees.

And Bailey was holding the phone again.

"Buttercup," he said softly. "What the fuck?"

"The paparazzi are stationed outside the apartment because of your mom's arrest." Her voice dropped. "Veronica got a little panicked about you guys being caught out in a crush."

A little.

Yeah, that was far from *a little*.

But there were more pressing topics to address.

Mainly, "My mother was arrested?"

Bailey's brows dragged together. "Did you *not* read my text?"

"I only looked at the preview," I said with a wince. "I saw *Everything is fine* and—" Another wince. "I didn't read the rest of it."

She huffed out a breath that was half annoyed and half amused. "*Helpful*, honey."

"Sorry, buttercup. In fairness"—my eyes cut to where Alex was still jumping on the trampoline, back-flipping like a champion now—"I didn't want to miss out on time with him."

Her expression went soft. "I know. But be forewarned, you might need to head back soon before the press figures out where you are."

"We'll head back to the car as soon as I get him his sourdough-shaped turtle."

A grin. "Softie."

I was. There was no doubt about that.

"He saw it through the window and since it wasn't a giant bag of candy or chocolate I thought—"

Bailey smiled. "I think it's a good thing, honey. Get him his treat and then"—she glanced over her shoulder and I saw that Veronica was still curled up into herself—"come home."

I nodded, saw that Alex was being lowered down, his feet now flat on the trampoline. "I need to go."

"Tell him awesome job on his backflips, yeah?"

Another nod.

Then she signed off.

Leaving me to retrieve Alex, to tell him that his mom and Bailey had seen those awesome backflips. Leaving me to get him that sourdough-shaped turtle.

Leaving me to try to focus on my son as the news she'd given me bounced around my head.

My mother arrested.

How had that happened?

I resisted the urge to shake my head, forced myself to focus on the convoluted tale that Alex was telling me about some fight that had broken out at school over who had the best sharpened pencil.

"And then Cassie held up her pencil and—"

That sounded more than a little bit dangerous, but I didn't comment on that, just listened, just tried not to focus on my mother, on *Alex's* mother, worry knotting itself in my belly.

Veronica had been *wrecked*.

I needed to find out why.

But first we had bread to buy, a car to return to, and...

Media to avoid.

THIRTY-FIVE

BAILEY

I turned back to Veronica, wondering how to approach the other woman.

She'd stopped crying, but the quiet that now filled her set my teeth on edge.

There was something wrong.

Something was very, *very* wrong.

I pocketed my cell. "They're going to head back," I said quietly.

A nod was the only sign that she heard me, her head still pressed up to her knees which were clutched to her chest, her arms wrapped tightly around her legs, fingers interlaced, knuckles standing out in sharp relief.

Now what?

I didn't know Veronica all that well, but this certainly wasn't what I was planning for our first foray into a Girl's Night In, and I wasn't all that sure she *wanted* my interference, wanted me to hobble my way over to her, to clumsily make my way down onto my ass next to her, Spock joining me and wriggling his soft, furry body in between us.

Because I couldn't leave her like that.

Despite my clumsy movements and cast that I was so fucking ready to get rid of, it wasn't even funny.

Something else that wasn't funny?

Whatever was happening to Veronica right now.

But I didn't push her, just sat there next to her, hoping that she would unfreeze if just given a little more time.

When she didn't after my ass started going numb, I realized that I was going to have to break the silence. Except, how to do that? Gently, like Veronica herself? Brashly, like the route Axel probably would have gone, shocking her out of her quiet (most likely by pissing her off until she broke)? Or...honestly, with the same kind of straight shooting that I appreciated?

I chose option three.

"Well, clearly something is wrong," I announced.

Veronica went somehow *more* still.

Then she looked up at me.

Thank fuck.

Though, her incredulous expression *did* make my lips curve, something that was probably inappropriate given that she'd been sobbing minutes before. Thankfully, though, she smiled in return, scrubbing a hand over her cheeks, and so I couldn't fault my tactics.

"Yes," she said with a half-hearted laugh, with a shake of her head. "Something is wrong."

I waited for her to expand on that statement.

When she didn't, I asked, "Well...um...want to clue me in on what that is?"

Her gaze went a little unfocused. "I was going to talk to you guys about it tonight." Her throat worked and I winced in solidarity to the painful swallow I bore witness to. "After Alex was asleep."

That didn't sound good.

And yeah, thank you, Captain Obvious.

I inhaled, exhaled. The apartment was only one bedroom, but we had a pullout sofa that Alex and Veronica had been staying on.

Not perfect, but considering we were just beginning the process of looking for a house near the city and the ranch would take a while to be rebuilt (and considering I still wasn't sure what form that rebuild would end up as—a big house? A barn? Something completely different because trying to recreate Gramps's and Gran's place might be too cripplingly painful?).

We had options.

But we'd decided to make those options with Alex and Veronica in mind.

That thought freshly drifting across my brain, I said, "We can wait until he is, if you want."

Her throat worked in that painful swallow again and her fingers threaded into Spock's fur, stroking him when he wiggled closer.

"No," she whispered. "I—I need to tell someone. I just..." A shake of her head. "I found out yesterday before we drove up, and I didn't really have time to process."

Process what? I wanted to ask.

Patience.

Thankfully, I didn't require a lot of it.

Because then she laid it out in a blunt sort of honesty I definitely appreciated...

Even as her words tore me to shreds.

———

She'd pulled herself together in record time, I thought. No evidence of the tears that had reignited and dripped down her cheeks as she'd told me what she'd learned before they'd made the drive up to Axel's apartment.

And the more I'd learned, the more I'd respected her.

How she'd held herself together for Alex...

Veronica might be gentle and sweet, but there was no doubt that there was a huge well of inner strength that she was able to draw from.

But she'd been drawing from that well for too long, and it was growing dry.

I watched as she smoothed her hand down Alex's back, the little boy having already eaten the turtle's head and two legs, along with some cheese and cold cuts and an apple. Not the healthiest or most gourmet of dinners but considering he hadn't wanted to partake in the Thai food I'd ordered after finding out it was Veronica's favorite, I thought it was a win. Protein, fruit, carbs, dairy. It hit most of the necessary food groups.

And considering I'd parted with one half of my favorite Crumbl cookie—and considering it was only rotated onto the menu at very infrequent intervals, that was akin to me sharing a once-in-a-lifetime treasure.

But...I loved the kid and he'd given me puppy dog eyes and what his mom had told me...

Well, he was going to need that cookie.

For now, though, I was killing some time reading in the bedroom—and by reading, I was basically scanning the same page over and over again, trying to make sense of the words...and not making any progress of it.

Axel, for his part, was practically vibrating as he reclined next to me.

He'd read Alex a chapter from a book I'd found in a local store, chronicling the trials and tribulations of a young horse finding his way in the world. And though it did something to me to watch him read to his son (and made my ovaries squeeze in a way they really never had before), I was as on edge as he was.

I'd intercepted him before he could pull Veronica aside, something he hadn't liked in the least.

But he'd listened to me, had banked his impatience and made it through dinner, through the movie (a rewatch of *Black Beauty* which had sung to my horse-crazy heart), through bath time and a round of *Sorry* and a chapter of that horsey book.

Soon, his patience would run out.

Though, I knew he'd wait until Alex was asleep, even if it *was* eating at him.

I set my book down, giving up on the page I clearly wasn't going to be able to process, and reached for his hand, lacing our fingers together.

"You know."

Two words, not accusatory, but his hand was holding mine tightly, his gaze locked with mine, trying to ferret out what I wasn't telling him. Not hurting me. Not trying to intimidate. Just...knowing that I knew and looking for hints of what it might be.

"Yeah," I said.

"And it's not good."

Now *I* was the one who was swallowing painfully, knowing that this was going to hurt Axel, going to hurt Alex, going to hurt Veronica.

"No," I murmured. "It's not good."

His fingers convulsed, lungs inflating, shoulders lifting and then falling, lungs deflating on the deep breath he took. "Okay."

This man that I loved had been through too damned much.

I hated that he was going to have to shoulder even more.

"We'll handle it together." My eyes drifting from his to Veronica, who'd stood up from the couch, who was crossing to the kitchen and sitting on one of the stools.

He pressed a kiss to the back of my hand, to my knuckles, and then he was reaching underneath me, scooping me up, carrying me across the apartment and settling me on a stool. Saving me from my crutches.

He didn't step away once I was steady, his front pressing to my back, one hand on the counter, the other on my hip.

Using *me* to steady him.

Trusting me.

And *that* was how I knew we'd be okay.

Even after Veronica told him her news.

THIRTY-SIX

AXEL

A little over a month later, I carried the last box into the guest house and looked around, pleased that we'd gotten this together so quickly.

The guest house was all flat, all one story.

Something that Veronica was going to need in the coming months.

That thought send the rage soaring through me all over again, a familiar wave that had been burning through me at regular intervals.

Because Veronica was sick.

She'd had a pain in her ribs, a persistent ache that she'd attributed to a strained muscle or getting older.

But when it hadn't gone away after several months, she'd gone in to see her doctor.

Who'd dismissed her complaints, prescribed her some painkillers, and told her when those ran out, to switch to ibuprofen.

V was a busy mom, had moved on, dealt with the pain for several more months. Until it had gotten so bad that the ibuprofen hadn't touched it and neither had the stronger medication that she hadn't bothered to take before.

That was six weeks ago.

That was when she'd gone to a different doctor.

That was when they'd found the cancer, news shared over the fucking phone with her before she'd made a six-hour drive up to the apartment I'd rented from Brit.

The thought of her sitting on that news, of her damp eyes as she'd told me she hadn't wanted to ruin my first full weekend with Alex in San Francisco had pretty much destroyed me. I loved her— in a way that was completely different from the way I loved Bailey, in a way that probably made me a fucking softie instead of, as Bailey liked to say, a big, broody hockey player, because I'd only known her a short amount of time and I loved her like a sister. But I also loved her in a way that was filled with respect and admiration and no little amount of guilt and regret. She'd given me Alex. She'd given *Alex* a good life. She'd been warm and vulnerable and open to letting me and Bailey both join in on Alex's life.

There was plenty to love about her.

"That's the last one," Bailey murmured, her arms full of several grocery bags as she moved to the fridge, finishing the stock up.

There were two bedrooms in the guest suite.

One for Veronica and one for Alex.

There was also a bedroom for Alex in the house and space for Veronica, as well, just in case she needed to be closer.

For now, I'd wanted to give her space.

Or, well, that had been Bailey's idea—to modify our house search to include space for both of them, to find the best doctors for the particular kind of cancer Veronica had been diagnosed with.

Kidney cancer that had metastasized to her lungs.

That rage flowed again, digging my fingers into the box, making me want to launch it across the room.

Noting that, I sucked in a breath, released it slowly, tucking that rage away—channeling it for future use on the ice. October couldn't come soon enough, and I'd sure as shit be burning through the anger during any ice time I could rustle up in the meantime.

Luckily, I had connections.

I carried the box into Veronica's bedroom, setting the box of sweaters in the closet.

She wouldn't need them for a few months, but she *would* need them, especially with the San Francisco fog drifting south of the big city and gathering in the hills where I'd bought this house. The evenings could get chilly in fall and winter, even in temperate California.

When I came out of the bedroom, Bailey was done with the fridge and shoving the canvas bags that had held the groceries into one another, stashing them in the cabinet next to the refrigerator.

She must have heard me come in because she straightened, took one look at me, and then she was crossing the space, wrapping her arms around me, making me thank fucking God that I had her in my life.

"Hey," she murmured, when I held her tight and didn't let her go for a long time.

"I'm fine."

A snort. Her not buying my bullshit.

Not ever.

Which was a good thing.

I don't know how I would have made it through all of this without her.

I wouldn't have. Bar none.

"I love you," I rasped.

"Those are some intense eyes, honey," she whispered, leaning back enough to bring her hands to my face. "And an intense declaration of your feelings."

"You've done—"

Her grip on my face tightened. "No more of that. You've thanked me a hundred times already. We love each other. We get our shit done together. I don't need your undying gratitude, honey. I just need you to keep loving me." Her mouth kicked up. "Okay, so maybe I also need your cock and fingers and tongue and all the ways they make me come, but"—her palm rested over my heart—"you have to breathe, to live right now. We're doing what we can for them both. We're going to keep doing that."

We were. I knew that.

Bailey had found the doctors and got Veronica in for treatment.

I'd found this house.

We were making them both a home. We were doing it together.

But...it wasn't easy for me to accept help, not even from the woman who owned me.

Something she knew because her mouth kicked up again. "Easy to say," she told me softly, raising up on tiptoe and brushing her lips over mine. "Hard to do. Especially for stubborn assholes like us."

"You're not an asshole."

Another brush of her lips, her hand skating down, drifting toward the waistband of my jeans. "Stop looking for an argument and come out front with me so we can doublecheck the moving truck and send them off. Alex and Veronica aren't coming in for a few hours, and I want to fuck you in our new house."

I inhaled.

Yeah, I wanted to fuck her in our house. Yeah, I wanted to use her body to forget.

We'd had precious little time for that between Alex and Veronica's illness and the season and the fire and her injuries and subsequent lengthy recovery—

Way too many fucking things getting between me and sinking into her lush, wet body.

So I let her dip her fingers beneath the waistband of my jeans, dance them across the already hardening ridge of my erection. I allowed her to indulge—and yeah, yeah, my life was *so* hard with my woman's hand wrapping around my cock—as I took her other hand, pressed my lips to the inside of her wrist, trailing them up along her inside of her elbow, knowing that was a spot that never *ever* failed to make her shiver.

Then, because we were indulging, I kissed her.

No brush of our lips.

But a melding of our mouths that took the rage inside me and transformed it into need that blistered along the insides of my veins, that threatened to make my knees weak, that had me drawing her flush to her body.

"Hey, we need to—"

I jerked my mouth away from Bailey's at the sound of the mover's voice trailing in through the open door, cock aching, mind fuzzy, rage trickling back in.

At being interrupted.

The mover cleared his throat, eyes deliberately not on me, not on Bailey.

Yeah, that was probably because I had my hand on her ass and the other one under her shirt and cupping her breast.

Bailey touched my jaw and I glanced down, saw that her eyes were dancing with amusement.

"You clear the truck"—her lips tipped up, and she squeezed my dick again, making me have to smother a groan, the fucking minx—"I'll meet you in the bedroom."

Proud of herself for the teasing, she slipped out of my hold, strutted—yes, *strutted*—to the door.

A flash of a brown ponytail.

A glimpse of that gorgeous, denim-clad ass I was desperate to be inside of.

The mover cleared his throat. "I..."

Right.

I needed to get rid of him.

And then I was going to fuck the woman I loved until she felt me inside her with every breath, every step, every heartbeat.

Poor, *poor* me.

THIRTY-SEVEN

I shivered, thinking of the look that Axel had shot me when I'd brushed my pelvis against his, the heat in his eyes threatening to turn my bones to jelly.

He was going to fuck me senseless...and I was here for it.

Lips twitching, I kicked off my shoes, not caring they ended up thumping against the wall, landing haphazardly on the wooden floor of our bedroom.

We'd moved our stuff over the previous week—not that Axel and I had a lot of furniture.

Mine had turned to ash, minus the horseshoe that Axel had saved for me.

Though, I supposed that couldn't be considered furniture. A knickknack. A keepsake. The one item that had survived the fire.

Axel'd had it framed, and that frame was currently living on my nightstand.

It always sent a pulse of joy to my heart and a pulse of pain.

But, even with the pain, I was so happy I had it, so touched—

I heard the rev of the moving truck's engine, and realized I was staring off into space, not taking advantage of this moment to prep the surprise I'd cooked up for Axel.

Well, it was for me too, something that would hopefully end with me having many, many orgasms.

I'd bought *supplies*.

"Why are you grinning?" he asked, making me jump as I'd bent over, intending to yank off my jeans.

Dammit. I'd daydreamed too long.

"Stay right there," I ordered. "I need to grab"—his hands came to my hips from behind, pelvis pressing to my ass, the hard jut of his erection almost exactly where I wanted it (minus the clothes between us)—"*hey!*" I snapped, trying to kick off my pants. "I need to grab—"

His palm slid up, under my bra, cupping my breast and plucking at my nipple.

Suddenly, I wasn't thinking about my *supplies*.

Because, oh God, his big, warm hand felt *divine*.

He rolled my nipple between thumb and forefinger, sending bolts of pleasure down my torso, coiling in my belly, gathering between my thighs. Then my bra and shirt disappeared and—

"Axel—"

"Hush," he murmured, pushing me forward—

And, oh look at that, I fell right onto the bed.

Hands skating down my spine, the backs of my legs, pausing to tug my jeans off my ankles.

They landed almost silently on the floor, but I wasn't paying attention to where they ended up, not when his hands were sliding back up, cupping my cheeks, massaging the sensitive globes.

"Fuck, this *ass*," he groaned, leaning forward and nipping one cheek, making me arch up and press that ass against his mouth.

His tongue flicked out, dragging over my skin, making me shiver as he used teeth and lips and, yes, that tongue to trace patterns, to kiss his way along my skin, my curves. His beard was the best type of abrasion, raising goose bumps on my arms, on my legs, pebbling my nipples, tightening them into stiff buds that rubbed against the comforter and made me gasp.

But I gasped again when he shoved my legs apart, his shoulders spreading me wide.

One long, slow flick of his tongue from my clit to the taut rosebud between the cleft of my cheeks.

"Honey—"

Fingers gripping my ass. "Hush," he ordered again.

And then his tongue...well, the things he did with it should have been illegal, one hand holding me still, keeping me against his mouth, the other slipping beneath me, teasing my breasts, sliding down to circle my clit.

Wet.

I was so *fucking* wet.

Then the tip of his tongue slid in.

I moaned, his name on my lips, my hips grinding back against him.

But he didn't stop, didn't show me any mercy.

My plan, my supplies, my thoughts of distracting him with pleasure, with enjoying our bodies, finding something pleasurable amongst all the things weighing us down had completely flown out of my mind.

I was a creature reduced to sensation, working myself against his tongue, his fingers.

Then I found myself up on my hands and knees, his big fingers inside me, my orgasm so, so close.

His tongue going deeper. His fingers thrusting faster.

And then my orgasm wasn't close.

It was barreling down on me, tearing through me, filling every single inch of me with pleasure, and swear to fuck, I blacked out for a moment.

I came to, still on my hands and knees, my body singing as his cock stroked through the wet folds of my pussy.

It was then that I remembered my supplies.

Sliding forward, even though I wanted nothing more than to arch my hips, to slot the head of his thick cock at my entrance and push back, to bring him inside me, to buck against him as he fucked me good and deep.

But...there were things I wanted to do, things we'd been talking about for months, things he'd been teasing me toward since almost the first time we were together.

Things he was preparing me for.

Just like he'd been doing with his tongue tonight.

"Buttercup," he growled.

I glanced over my shoulder at him, watching his eyes drift up from my ass, my pussy, up to my breasts—or at least the side of one, a view he'd told me more than once that he enjoyed.

And today, tonight, I felt the heat of his stare traveling through my breast, my nipple, pleasure coiling, taunting me, calling me to move back to him, to spread my legs and prepare to be fucked. Shivering with need, I crawled to my nightstand, reached for the drawer and pulled out my *supplies*.

Heat had been warring with a scowl on his face, but when he saw what I'd retrieved that heat went molten.

He crawled up next to me, sliding a hand all along my side, up and down and *in*. "You trying to tell me something, buttercup?"

"I think I already told you."

His hand didn't stop that slow and easy trek. "You sure?"

I leaned in, nipped the underside of his jaw, the bristles of his beard teasing my skin. "I brought the lube and toys, didn't I?"

Those hot eyes stayed glued on mine as his nostrils flared.

Then he gave me a smile that I felt deep inside me, stroking through me, just like his fingers and tongue had. "You did at that, buttercup."

I opened my mouth to reply but didn't manage to get any words out.

Because Axel had turned into a whirlwind.

His mouth hit mine for a scorching kiss that stole all the air in my lungs, then it was moving over my body—along my throat, my breasts, my belly, *lower*. Using my supplies to take slick folds and make them even more wet, his finger drawing through that dampness, dragging it back, pressing it in.

One finger.

Two.

Three.

All while his tongue and lips worked me. All while his free hand roved over my body, teasing my breasts, rolling my nipples, dragging down to circle my clit.

When he used the toy I'd bought, I found I couldn't breathe, couldn't think, could hardly concentrate on sensation as pleasure flowed through me, whipped me into a frenzy, sent my mind to haze, my body to a trembling mass that needed...

Oh God, it *needed*.

As though he'd heard me, and hell, maybe I'd said it aloud, maybe I'd begged him, maybe I'd gasped out to "Please! Get *inside* me," he slipped the toy free and reached for the lube, rubbing it over the hard length of his erection, turning the crown of him slick and shiny, even as the fingers of his other hand slipped back inside me and flexed, stretching me, preparing me, driving me wild.

"Buttercup?" he asked.

I managed to tear my eyes open, saw him poised between my legs.

"Yes," I said, assuring him again that I was there with him.

His fingers slid out, wrapped around his cock, and his pressed gently against that tight, *tight* rosebud nestled deep in the cleft of my ass.

I gasped at the slight burn, at the stretch, gasped as the muscles gave way and he was suddenly partway in.

He stopped. "Bailey."

"*No*," I moaned.

But then I realized what that sounded like because he started to pull out, saying, "It's okay—"

"*No!*" I moaned again, eyes finding his. "It's good." I shifted hesitantly against him, wanting him deeper, needing him fully inside. "I need more. I need *you.* "

His jaw going tense, eyes flaring with heat.

And then he was pressing in deeper, that burn expanding, leaving me feeling so fucking full that I could barely think, especially when he slid two fingers inside my pussy, his thumb coming up to rub my clit.

I moaned.

"Fuck, honey," he groaned, stilling when he was fully in, my pussy clenching around his fingers, my hips shifting. Needing him to move.

"Move, please," I begging, arching against him. "Fuck. Please, just fuck me."

He did—with cock and fingers, with lips and teeth and tongue.

And—

My pussy convulsed.

He grew bigger inside me, his strokes losing their steady, controlled rhythm as he teetered toward the edge.

But that was okay, because I was the balance beam of pleasure myself—one touch, one breath, one stroke away from falling off.

His lips closed over my nipple, sucked just a bit too hard.

And that bit of pleasure-pain sent me falling.

Distantly, as bliss flowed through every inch of me, I heard his rough grunt, my name tumbling off his tongue, the strokes going hard and haphazard and *wild*.

I held on to him as we both came down to Earth, with arms and legs and *heart*, this wicked man who made me trust him with every part of me.

Who'd never abused that trust.

Who'd showed me so much more than I ever could have imagined.

My lips curved as my brain slowly cleared, as I came to sprawled across his chest, his hands gentle as he held me.

I giggled.

He tensed, hand stilling.

"You okay?" he asked carefully.

I pressed up enough to see his face, my smile growing. "I can't wait for you to corrupt me some more."

He gave me his most sinful smile, the one that never failed to make me melt. "Who would have thought I'd corrupt the woman who pointed a shotgun at me and ordered me off her porch?"

I giggled again, buried my face in his throat, knowing that I'd have many more years of his corruption ahead. "Well," I said, pressing my lips to his skin, my fingers trailing through the silk of his hair. "It *did* start with handcuffs."

His laughter after so many weeks of tension and darkness was the best gift he'd ever given me.

Aside from the orgasms, that was.

Thirty-Eight

We were both limp and dozing when the doorbell rang.

Eyes wide, we looked at each other, pushed off the bed and hustled for our clothes strewn around the room.

Or at least, I was.

Bailey had snagged her robe, was shrugging into it, knotting the tie around her waist.

I paused, my jeans unbuttoned and hanging on my waist. "Umm..."

"Not it." She grinned. "I'm due for a nice hot bath."

Her eyes.

Fuck, the naughtiness in them, the unspoken "Yeah, you made me dirty," had my cock twitching, my fingers itching to get her dirty again, to corrupt her some more.

I'd taken a step toward her.

Only the doorbell rang again.

Groaning, I ran to the bathroom and rushed through washing

up, skidding to a halt back in front of her a few moments later, giving in to the urge to kiss her until my lungs burned.

We broke apart and I brushed my knuckles over her cheek.

"Be down in a bit," she murmured.

I squeezed her ass. "See that you do."

"Be down in a while," she replied, sassing me without hesitation.

I loved it. I loved *her*.

"*Terror*."

A nip to my bottom lip. "Damn right." Then she turned for the bathroom.

I swatted her ass before she managed to make it out of reach—the one I just about killed myself fucking not long before, every single one of my fantasies nowhere near comparable the way she'd felt, how she'd lit up for me, the smirk she'd given me when she'd come on my fingers and cock.

I couldn't wait to do it again, wanted to follow her right into the bathroom and coax her into another round.

But...

The door.

She blew me a kiss, disappeared into the bathroom.

Growling, I tugged my shirt over my head and then I hustled down the stairs.

But any bit of irritation left my body when I opened it and Alex threw himself into my arms, shouting, "Dad!"

Because the rest of my family was here.

And, later, after Bailey emerged from the bath, damp curls of hair clinging to cheeks that were flushed pink from the heat, joining in on the board game in progress without missing a beat, her body leaning against mine, her hand on my thigh and her laughter in the air, I was settled in a way I'd never anticipated.

The love of a good woman.

Friends who were better than blood.

My son, who brought utter fucking joy to my heart, and his mom, who was wonderful in her own right.

This was all right.

Because *all* of my family was here.

———

The next couple of weeks were filled with plenty of good.

It was awesome having Alex there, and the more that I got to know my son, the more I liked him. He had a big heart, rarely lost his temper, showed kindness to everyone, and had so much energy that we'd started going on daily hikes.

Easy because the house backed up to green space.

Great because it gave us time to get to know each other and drain that energy that never seemed to wane.

Terrible because the kid was turning into a marathoner—running up the trail, keeping just to the edge of my sight. Sprinting back down to me, taking my hand and dragging me along even as he chatted my ear off somehow without getting out of breath. Then he'd get impatient with my slow and steady pace (me, as a professional hockey player, trying to not let my son show me up because the kid had *energy*) and run off to do it all again.

We'd found him a soccer team.

He'd been folded right into the Gold crew, right into the gaggle of kiddos who were always around the team, had regular playdates, had gone to the summer camp the team put on.

Friends and sports and other activities—and plenty of time at the Dairy.

He'd discovered his love of soft serve and running under the strings of lights hanging in the large oak trees.

See? Boundless energy?

But all of that good had been tempered with bad.

Veronica had begun treatment, and though she'd been fine for the first couple of weeks, those treatments were now taking their toll on her.

She was pale, sleeping a lot, and no matter how many hikes Alex and I went on, it wasn't going to make it any easier for our son.

Case in point, the call I'd just gotten.

The reason I was heading to the rink to pick him up from summer camp.

He'd punched someone.

My kind son with the big heart had punched one of the other campers.

I should have kept him home today. I'd debated the action just that morning, knowing that he'd heard Veronica being sick for much of the night, that we couldn't hide how terrible she was feeling from him, not when they were so close.

But we'd—V, Bailey, and I—had a quick chat about it that morning, had decided that normalcy was better.

Now, I knew that was the wrong call.

Sighing, I turned off the ignition and opened my door, trying to be all mature and shit, knowing that I wasn't going to always make the right parenting decision, that I was going to fuck up.

But shit, this didn't feel good.

"Neither does he, asshole," I muttered, slamming the door and heading to the ring of tree trunks where I could see Alex and a counselor sitting.

My son's swollen and reddened eyes killed me.

The counselor tilted his head, and I followed him a little distance away, got the briefing of what had gone down, and felt my own rage well up, felt the need to punch the little shit of a kid myself. Unfortunately, I had to be a grownup.

Nodding when the counselor informed me the other kid wouldn't be welcome back because he refused to apologize, even after Alex had shown genuine remorse for his outburst. And considering what the little shit had said, I appreciated the teens and young adults running the camp taking a stand for my son, and knowing what he was going through, showing support rather than holding to hard lines of discipline.

Not that violence was ever the right answer.

But verbal abuse could be just as bad.

"Alex is welcome back tomorrow," the young man said, "so long as he keeps his hands to himself."

I nodded. "Thanks. I'll talk to him, see what he wants to do."

The counselor disappeared back around the side of the building where I could hear young voices yelling and screaming and generally having a great time.

Now I had to figure out how to handle this.

Once that thought would have paralyzed me. I was young, hadn't had a dad, hadn't really had a mom, how would *I* make the right choice? But I wasn't alone...I'd had good coaches, I'd watched my teammates, internalized their parenting choices, banking it to use later, to use in times like these.

Not that they were perfect.

But I'd learned from them.

And I'd built the beginnings of a bond with my son. He trusted me. Of course, we'd mostly just had fun times so who knew if I'd make the right call here—

"And you're stalling, dumbass," I muttered, inhaling and exhaling in a way that settled my nerves.

I was stalling.

Time to stop that shit.

Shoring myself up, I moved over to Alex and sat on the log next to him.

He didn't make me wait for it, didn't make me *work* for it, just turned to me with those red, swollen eyes and said, "I'm a bad person."

A knife to my heart.

"No, buddy," I told him quickly. "You're not bad. You made a mistake."

His bottom lip quivered, but he didn't say anything, just looked away from me, shoulders hunching more.

And, hell, I went with my instincts and scooped him up, drawing him into my lap, wrapping him tight in my arms. "You were wrong to punch him," I said, hating that his little body grew even more stiff at my words. "But you already know that, yeah?"

A tense moment of silence.

Then a very, *very* slight nod. "Yeah," he whispered.

"You can come back to camp tomorrow," I told him. "As long as you keep your hands to yourself." His stiff body didn't relax. "Barker won't be allowed back."

Shock had Alex's head shooting up, eyes wide.

"They know what he said." I cupped the back of his head, his hair silk on my palm. "So I get the urge," I told him, allowing my mouth to quirk up, just slightly, thinking that he needed a little light after being forced to face a fact that we'd all been trying to protect him from. "But even with the provocation, you can't go around punching people."

"You do it on the ice," he pointed out.

Smart kid. Too fucking smart for his own good.

"True, but even on the ice we get punished."

Alex considered that, nodded. "I want to come back tomorrow," he said. "They're making tie-dye shirts and they said I could make one for Mom."

Kind. Sweet. A growing spine of steel.

Alex was going to be a good, good man one day.

Now, he was young, a kid who was learning and making mistakes and fuck—

"I love you," I said fiercely, hugging him close.

He wrapped his arms around my middle, squeezed me tight. "I don't want Mom to die."

That was what the little shit of the kid had said, what had triggered my kind, caring son (with the spine of steel) into getting physical.

Shattering a barrier we'd been trying to keep in place.

One he had probably already been smart enough to see behind.

One that had probably hurt anyway, because we'd all been trying to focus on that not being a possibility.

But it was.

The cancer was serious.

The treatment was too.

Veronica had a long road ahead of her.

And that road might not lead to living a full and healthy life and—

Alex sniffed.

Fuck, I hated this for V, for Alex, for all they might lose.

But I couldn't lie to him, couldn't pretend that it *wasn't* a possibility, wouldn't insult his intelligence by pretending his worry wasn't a reality.

We could lose her.

So, all I said was, "I know. I don't want to lose her either."

And then I held him while he cried, those tears soaking through my shirt, and when he was able to stop, when he looked up at me again, I threaded my fingers through his hair, kissed the top of his head, reminded him, "She's going to fight for us, bud. Let's make sure to do the same for her." Though, his intent nod had me tacking on, "Minus punching."

Alex's mouth curved and then he was giggling, those giggles turning to shrieks when I stood up, taking him with me, tossing him over my shoulder and jogging to my car.

And because we were already on the right side of town, we hit the Dairy.

Because hugs and jokes, crying and being held, I'd learned how important all of those could be to feeling better. And because of the Gold, because of Bailey, I'd also learned in-depth about the healing properties of soft serve.

Especially, when it was mixed with cookie crumbs and peanut butter and lots and lots of chocolate syrup.

THIRTY-NINE

BAILEY

T he wind was weaving through the short grass, giving me that soft *shush* of sound that I had missed so *fucking* much.

It wasn't what it once had been, the noise quiet instead of ringing through my ears.

But it was a touch of peace, a sign of regrowth.

The town was coming back.

And so was the ranch.

I inhaled, happy to find that for the first time since I'd come back to town, there was not one whisper of smoke and ash and destruction on the air.

Just...home.

Though, now, I could comfortably say that I had *several* homes —the ranch, the house Axel and I were living in with V and Alex, the sun and wind and sky, and Axel.

He was my home, too.

Though, it was funny. Because V and Alex had become such a

big part of my home too, even though it was all so new, I couldn't imagine life without them.

"I'm not surprised that you've bonded with them so tightly already."

I blinked at my aunt, her blond curls shining bright in the early afternoon sunshine. It was blazing hot, and I was sweating. I knew that soon enough we were going to head back for the air-conditioned interior of the car, that we'd head to downtown and buy a meal at one of the newly reopened restaurants—supporting another facet of my family, of my home. But for now, I was enjoying watching Veronica sitting on a blanket, soaking in the heat when she'd spent so much time feeling cold since her treatments had begun. I was enjoying watching Alex run around the field.

Axel was talking to the contractor I'd hired, the pair of us having already walked through the stakes and flags and bright pinkish-orange tape that had been strung, denoting the two houses we were going to build, the barn that was going to come up.

My herd was in the hills, greatly reduced in number in a way that had brought tears to my eyes, but it was also bigger than before because I'd taken on the remaining head of cattle from my neighbors. Not up here as often as I would like, I'd had the fences rebuilt and was paying some local teens to check the fencing and put out hay.

They were healthy and well-fed and okay for the moment, and with the remnants of Tom, Hank, and Eli's herds the expense wasn't cheap.

But...their memories were alive in that way. And for the moment, I couldn't part with them.

"What do you mean?" I asked, focusing on her, on the comment she'd made. "It's not exactly a well-kept secret that I'm not great at letting people in."

Billie snorted. "The issue was never letting people *in*." A nudge of my shoulder. "It was the hurt they caused once they *were* in."

My aunt had always had a gift at seeing right through me.

It was annoying at the best of times, heart-rending at others.

But together it struck true and deep, and I narrowed my eyes at her. "That's just mean."

It was too close to the freaking truth, too close to bringing up memories of the people who'd hurt me—the people who'd hurt me over and over. No. Not people. They were supposed to have been my family, two by blood, one by marriage, and they'd instead they'd left me wounded.

Thank God they weren't in my life any longer.

"It's the truth," she said.

And it was.

I'd spent plenty of time looking back and locking myself in my own head, burying the needs of my heart.

I didn't do that anymore.

Not since a certain interfering aunt had made it her mission to make that task impossible.

"Annoying," I muttered, since I couldn't deny that she *was* speaking the truth.

"Stubborn."

"Takes one to know one," I grumbled, sticking my tongue out at her.

A begrudging sigh. "Unfortunately you speak the truth."

"Is it a truth that I should be speaking to *Joel* about?" Did I draw out his name? Hell, yeah, I did. My aunt was hell on wheels, and Joel wasn't much better. They'd spent more time than not sniping at each other—and it was a well-known fact that Joel's nickname for Billie was harpy.

Not that I would necessarily say it was well *deserved*, but then again...it wasn't out of the realm of possibility.

"Annoying," *she* muttered, taking a page out of my book. "And for my nosy niece, we called a truce right about the time the town burned down. Not that I've seen much of him since we were able to move out of the shelter."

The edgy statement was more than a little prickly and it sent a note of understanding down my spine.

Hmm.

But, as I'd said, my aunt was hell on wheels, and she wasn't easily distracted.

Not even by a certain annoying hockey player who liked to push her buttons and call her a harpy.

Her palm rested on my cheek for a moment, sliding down to cup my jaw. "Back to the people who *matter*— "

"Ah."

She frowned.

"Apparently delusion is a family trait."

Billie Rose went still for a long moment.

Then she glared at me. "You always *have* been a pain in my ass." She brought her other hand up, holding both sides of my face and freezing me in place with piercing blue eyes. "What I'm trying to say is that they're vulnerable. You spent too much time feeling the same growing up to let anyone in your vicinity feel the same, especially when they're innocent."

I sucked in a breath.

"Even if that innocent is an unexpected child and baby mama."

My breath slid out on a hiss, a kernel of outrage in my heart. I didn't like the insinuation. Not at all. It was something that had been made too often during the time we'd spent getting our fifteen minutes of fame. Veronica was only one-half of what had happened. Axel bore responsibility too. And Clarice, well, that bitch owned more than her fair share of blame.

Especially since she'd been released from jail pending those charges and had spent the majority of her time denigrating Axel and Veronica (and me! Go me!) on social media. Though, Colt had been kind enough to give an interview as well.

Flattering, it hadn't been.

But he was my ex for a reason and I'd had my say with him.

So, we'd all ignored the blip in coverage that came from him getting his few minutes of fame off of Axel's...then I had deter-minedly changed the channel.

I'd done the same when my parents made the rounds.

Because, clearly, they hadn't wanted to miss an opportunity to rake in funds.

Luckily, neither they or Colt had gained much traction and ignoring them had been relatively easy.

Too bad we couldn't lock them up and throw away the key.

Alas, at least for Clarice, while she was annoying, she wasn't a violent criminal, so we had to deal with her having her freedom, as temporary as it may be.

"Alex and Veronica are great," I said, focusing on the positive.

"Yeah, they are." Billie tossed me arch look. "But the reason you're not threatened is because you know what it's like to be innocent and vulnerable and would never willingly subject anyone to the same fate."

"I'm not a saint."

"No," Billie said with a smile. "Though, it is easier to be open to said son and baby mama when your man looks at you like *that.*"

Her gaze slid to the side, mine following and immediately all of the air seized in my lungs.

Because my man was heading my way and the look on his face...

Ho. Mama.

Heat curled in my stomach, moisture gathering between my thighs, dampening my panties.

Something he knew, based on the way his lips turned up into a smirk. Our sex life...was *fire*. It had been great before, but now that my injuries were healed and my cast was off and we were spending so much time together because it was the off-season (something that would be ending soon, since he had to start training and getting back into ice-ready shape in the coming weeks), our sex life had transformed from heat and soaking up orgasms (not a bad thing) to intimacy and explorations and, yes, plenty of orgasms.

Hence, the smirk.

Hence me creaming my panties.

"Buttercup," he murmured, pulling me back against his chest.

"Did you get your manly time in with the contractor?" I teased.

I'd thought the run-through was more than thorough, but Axel had so many questions and kept the contractor here for so long, that I'd ended up calling Billie and she'd come out to kill some time while catching up before dinner.

He kissed the top of my head. "Have to make sure my family" —a nip to the top of my ear—"my *woman* is looked after."

"You do that already," I murmured, turning in the circle of his arms, throwing mine around his neck. I kissed him because he was mine and I could and he was here and—

"Geez," Billie grumbled. "Don't you get enough of that?"

"Never," I said against his lips.

A sound of disgust.

Then one of outrage.

Which—geez herself—I thought *that* was taking things a little far. I was just kissing my man.

Then I heard gravel crunching behind me, turned to see Joel's truck pulling into the driveway.

Ah. That was the cause of my aunt's outrage.

I glanced up at Axel, lifting my brows.

He just leaned close, lips finding my ear, his words hot and damp on my skin. "Payback for the handcuffs."

I burst out laughing...

Just as Joel strolled up.

FORTY

AXEL

"I oughtta smack you for putting me in the harpy's crosshairs again," Joel grumbled, winding up, ready for the puck I slid to him.

I passed.

He shot.

The crack of the stick on the ice ringing in my ears, ringing through the rink.

It was quiet, late in the evening, after all the games and practices and summer camps had wrapped up. Now, it was just me and Joel and Ryan on the empty sheet of ice. We'd even traded a signed puck with the ice attendant and had managed to get the ice cleaned of extra snow, the thin layer of water smoothed over the surface thanks to the Zamboni.

Now we had our skates and gloves (and helmets because, as Bailey had reminded all of us when she'd dropped us at the rink, we each only had one brain, and just because we decided not to use it sometimes, it was still something we should probably preserve) on and were fucking around, my woman's tart teasing still in my ears, still tucked close to my heart. God, I loved it when she sassed me.

I couldn't wait to smack her ass in punishment because of it.

Knowing I was grinning and not giving a fuck because my woman was fucking awesome, I just passed Joel another puck.

He shot.

It hit the top corner of the net.

I lined up another pass, prepared to send it over.

"I don't know," I said. "I think you've got something"—I slid the puck across—"going with the hot mayor."

Joel was mid-shot when my words reached him and his follow-through went wonky.

The puck missed the net by a fucking mile.

Grinning for a whole other reason now, I knew Joel well enough to easily duck the glove he chucked at my head. It hit Ryan, though, who stuffed it full of some snow that we'd managed to chew up on the ice from our fucking around.

Joel was too busy glaring at me to notice Ryan's antics.

But I saw him working out of the corner of my eyes.

And decided to give him more time to work some magic.

"Those curls," I said. "They taunt a man to tug on them, to see what they'd look like when they're straight...to see *where* they'd reach when she's naked." I smirked. "Maybe down to those breast—"

This time I didn't duck fast enough to avoid the glove.

Mostly because Joel might be a giant, but when he wanted to move quickly...he could.

Case in point, my teasing being cut off by eating the worn leather of his glove. "Bailey's gonna chop off your dick if she hears you talking about another woman's breasts," he said with a glower.

"She's related to Bailey." I shrugged. "I can appreciate the assets that come from shared DNA without getting in trouble."

Joel glared. "You're so full of shit."

"Yeah." I grinned. "I am."

And with perfect timing, Ryan pounced, dumping the glove full of snow right over the top of Joel's head.

Now, Joel was used to hockey players, used to the shit-giving that we dished out on a regular basis, but he was on edge from my teasing, on edge from whatever was brewing between him and Billie Rose, and he had a temper—slow-growing and not easy to ignite, but once it did, it fucking *erupted*.

Like it did in that moment as the snow was sliding down his face.

He growled and shot forward, taking me to the ice, then whipping around and taking Ryan down to the cold, hard surface in a movement that was so fast I could barely track it.

Then he was back, shoving my face into the ice, spinning and doing the same with Ryan.

I found my feet, danced away, laughter in my chest that was bubbling up and escaping so intensely that I bent at the waist, hands on my knees, and then I couldn't stand, couldn't keep those feet I'd found. I collapsed back down to the ice, the cool seeping into me.

Luckily, Joel's temper burned out quickly.

Probably because Ryan was laughing his ass off too, the noise our amusement was making even louder than our shots had been.

Joel balled up some snow, launched it at me. "Fucker," he grumbled and tossed it.

The cold, wet stuff exploded on my chest, soaking into my T-shirt.

It didn't bother me.

I was here with my friends, who'd stayed over at my house the night before. Veronica had finished her first round of treatment and even though she was still weak and had lost her hair, the doctors were feeling positive.

Dodging another snowball, I started to get to my feet again. At least I could get out of throwing distance.

But as I started to skate away, my gaze was drawn to movement near the glass windows leading out to the lobby of the rink. A flash of color, of blond. I blinked, looked closer, but it was gone. The games and practices and public skate times had concluded for the day, but workers were still around. Probably one of them wondering when the idiots (that being me and Joel and Ryan) were going to get off the ice sheets.

I started to turn back but realized my distraction had proved a critical error.

The fuckers—also known as my friends—had snuck up on me.

"Fuck!"

Half-melted snow ended up down my T-shirt, trapped between the fabric and my skin and making me jump like a fucking rabbit across the ice as I tried to get it out.

Which, of course, had the effect of turning Joel and Ryan into goddamned hyenas, cackling as they sprawled out on the cold surface.

"Assholes," I muttered, standing there.

Then deciding to pay them back, I backed up a few steps, took off and skated toward them full bore, stopping an inch from Joel's side and—I smiled with pride—showering them with snow. "Fuck—*ah!*"

Hell, my ass was going to be covered in bruises the next day, I knew.

That knowledge didn't stop my fall to the ice (head protected by the helmet, though, thankfully) and I ended up sprawled next to my friends, next to my former teammates.

All of us were out of breath, soaking wet, and still laughing like the idiots we were.

And I didn't care.

Because these assholes were part of my family too.

"I think that we were actually supposed to do more than shoot a couple of pucks and roll around on the ice," Ryan said once we'd sort of regained control of ourselves—or weren't laughing our assess off anyway.

"Meh," Joel said. "I needed to blow off some steam."

I scooted out of arm's reach. "Because you can't stop thinking about Billie Rose's breasts."

Joel's head swiveled toward me. Then back to Ryan. "I'm going to kill him."

Ryan stood up, brushed off his hands. "I'll hold him down for you."

And then we were off again.

Being idiots.

But fuck, it was fun.

Later, still soaked to the bone because we hadn't bothered to bring a change of clothes when we'd just planned on "fucking around with a few pucks," we let ourselves quietly into the house, having decided to take a Lyft back, since it was late and I didn't want to disturb Bailey.

Speaking of which, my woman smiled up at me, her legs curled up beneath her on her chair, her book laid out over its arm.

She lifted a finger, pressed it to her lips and I saw that Veronica was sleeping on the couch.

Pale and thin, a silk scarf wrapped around her hair.

There was a blanket tucked up beneath her chin and the lights were dimmed.

Bailey rose in the fluid, graceful way that made her so beautiful to watch on horseback, crossing to us as we quietly stashed our shit in the mud room. "I was going to see if you could carry her to her bed. But"—her gaze drifted down his torso, no doubt taking in his soaked shirt—"I see that you've"—spinning on her feet, seemingly looking at his former teammates—"all been getting into trouble."

"I'll go change and bring her over, buttercup." I wrapped an arm around her middle, drew her back against me, knowing that I was getting her wet and not caring.

Because then *she'd* have to change.

Just call me an evil genius.

Bailey narrowed her eyes at me, communicating that she saw right through me.

"I'll take her," Ryan said. "My shirt's mostly dry."

"Thanks, Ry," Bailey murmured, ass rubbing lightly against my hips. "Alex is in his room in the guest house, so do you mind carrying her out there?"

A shake of his head. "I'll do it now."

There was something about his...well, it wasn't eagerness exactly and I was probably overthinking this interaction, considering that Ryan was a much nicer guy than I was. Still, this didn't sit right with me. Veronica was vulnerable and—

Bailey rubbed against me.

A bit more deliberately this time and I ran my fingers over her hip, my cock deciding that it was time to get her out of her *wet* clothes. And anyway, Ryan was already slipping his arms beneath Veronica's body and Joel was opening the door and Bailey was taking my hand, tugging me toward the stairs.

Yeah, my cock had the right idea.

Definitely.

FORTY-ONE

"More wine, wench," Dessie demanded.

I glared at her, even though I was in the process of opening the bottle of wine to make a round of refills.

I wasn't buzzed enough for the collective Girl's Night that was Brit and Dessie and Billie Rose, but after our last Girl's Night had hit the rails (arrests and panic attacks and cancer diagnosis sharing hadn't made for all that fond of memories), I'd wanted to keep the circle tight, even while expanding on V and me.

I'd just...underestimated the collective force of this trio.

Or, as Veronica was proving, the quad.

V was quiet on first meeting, but she had an inner strength that shone through, and add in a shyness that faded with a glass or two of wine, along with getting to know someone better, and I was in for a wild ride.

Brit had brought *Ticket to Ride.*

Bad reality TV about people seeking sister wives was playing on the television and making me cringe even as I couldn't look away.

And we were all sharing.

And by sharing, I meant *sharing*.

I'd learned far too much about my aunt that evening.

Including, that those handcuffs—*both* of the pairs she'd used to keep Axel on my porch—had been used.

"Serving wenches in this tavern are slow," Dessie called.

My friend knew plenty about serving. She was a bartender at Monroe's—one of the restaurants (well, bar *and* restaurants) that had recently reopened. She was still being annoying...and I couldn't wait to copiously use the word *wench* the next time I was up in River's Bend.

"I'm trying to drink enough to burn the memory of my *aunt* and her enjoyment of being handcuffed from my mind," I yelled over the din.

Veronica tossed me a smile over her shoulder, her brightly patterned scarf tied in place on her head. "Don't knock cuffs until you try them."

I groaned. "Don't side with *her*," I accused. "She'll be unbearable now."

V's smile didn't fade and her response was nonverbal—holding up her empty glass.

I shoved in the bottle opener. "Okay, okay," I muttered, yanking out the cork. "This wench is getting to work."

"Just saying," Billie Rose said, coming over and plucking the bottle from my hand. She topped off glasses as she studied the board of *Ticket to Ride* with laser focus, no doubt planning her next move that would take them all out. "Sometimes the best type of sex is when you're able to give up control to a partner you trust."

I knew all about *that*.

Just that morning Axel had bent me into a position I hadn't thought was going to possible to hold, let alone be pleasurable, but, swear to fuck, the orgasm he'd given me as he'd pounded oh so slow and deep might have been the strongest one ever.

"Can we talk about anything that isn't sex-related?" I groused, grabbing one of the beers Axel and I had picked up from the microbrewery in town.

The boos came from all around on the heels of my statement and, ignoring them, I popped the top, rounded the island and headed back to my recliner.

Yup. I'd licked it.

It was mine.

Smothering my grin, because that licking had been the result of an accident. I'd been trying to lick my way up a certain big, broody hockey player's body, and I'd overshot.

Big dick problems.

Heh.

"Did you hear back about enrollment for the fall semester?" V asked, and boos aside, I appreciated her throwing me a bone.

"Yes," I said, nerves prickling in my belly. "I got into the program."

For teaching.

My prerequisites were in order for the most part. I had two more courses that I needed to complete, but I had wanted to do them concurrently. One tough year to get my training. Pass the CBEST. Complete my student teaching.

And then...

A dream I'd thought wouldn't ever happen would be within my grasp.

Because of Axel and Billie and Brit and Dessie and so many other people who'd stepped in and shown me the value of *me*.

And because *I'd* finally realized I was deserving of it.

Veronica grinned widely and put her glass down, reaching over the table (and jostling the pieces on the game board, much to Billie's consternation) to hug me tight. "I'm so happy for you!"

"Thanks," I said, hugging her back.

Then the conversation turned toward other things—TV, team gossip that Brit was somehow still keeping apprised of, despite her retired state, *town* gossip that Billie Rose was definitely on top of because she always knew everything about everyone. We talked about Veronica's job and how her boss had finally approved her for a full remote position and then briefly about the next steps for her treatment. It was good news and a step in the right direction—the doctors were pleased that they'd managed to stop the cancer from growing, and the next round would be focused on getting it to shrink. So, the right direction, but not necessarily easy.

No surprise, I was knocked out of the game early.

I'd like to blame it on all my daydreaming about Axel and the orgasms he gave me, but really, the other women were just much better than me.

Well, that, and I was also all in on seeking those sister wives.

There was much drama and much disbelief (how could they think of sharing their man?) and then there was much teasing from Billie, Brit, and Dessie about V and I being sister wives ourselves.

Which, I had to admit, made me reconsider.

Not sharing Axel, but our living arrangements and what those women on the screen must be seeking.

Look at me, taking off my judgy hat.

Eventually, we changed to a cooking show, and started doing the normal thing that people do when partaking in cooking challenges—talked about how much better we could make that particular dish. Judgy hat right back on.

Our disapproval aside, it was getting late, and pretty soon Billie and Dessie headed up.

They'd originally been planning on staying the night, but Billie had a meeting early in the morning, so they'd decided to just go home tonight.

I walked them to their car, got a hug from Dessie, a palm on my cheek from my aunt and a soft, "I'm proud of you about school," that had my eyes tearing up. By then Brit came strolling out, all long lines and bright smile.

She bleeped the locks on her car, squeezed me tight as Dessie backed out of my driveway, and declared that next Girl's Night was at her place...

And with the rest of the crew.

And that Dessie and Billie were invited.

Heaven help Veronica and me.

Grinning with that thought—because it would be fun, no matter how many people were there—I moved back into the house. Time for a soak in the tub, a fresh beer, and a fresh book. I was in the middle of a spicy romance series that had both been keeping me up late at night and also serving as inspiration for me with my man.

More orgasms, muahaha!

After letting Spock out to the back yard to do his business, I came back inside and checked the living room for anything left to clean, not finding anything because the girls had already cleared up before they'd taken off, and then was heading for the stairs when the doorbell rang.

Thinking one of those knuckleheads had left something behind, I tugged open the front door.

And sighed.

It had all been going so perfectly—wine and teasing, junk food and trash TV, hanging out and talking about important things (and plenty of non-important ones).

But now, looking at fucking *Candi* standing on my doorstep, I knew that I'd relaxed too soon.

I gripped the door, started to step outside, hoping to keep her away from Veronica...

Who chose that exact moment to walk into the hall, asking, "Who was there—?"

Candi lifted her arm.

Pointed her gun at me.

Fucking Girls' Nights.

Forty-Two

Axel

The lights were on in the family room when I stepped through the door from the garage, using my foot to push the door wide.

Because Alex had passed out on the way home.

His head was nestled into my neck, limp arms hanging down over my chest, his trusting, relaxed body taking up the rest of my arms.

I caught the door with my toe.

The kid would sleep through a lot, but I wasn't sure about slamming doors, so I let it shut softly, nudged it closed with my hip, and then did some more of the shifting that had enabled me to get in the house to lock the door.

A flick turned off the lights in the family room, and then I was carrying him down the hall, to the bedroom he had in the main house—this one was decorated with horses, his one in the guest house plastered with merch from his favorite YouTubers.

He slept in both equally, though, he always slept in this one if Veronica was sleeping in the main house.

Tonight, I helped him use the bathroom, tugged off his shoes, then tucked him in the bed, seeing that the door to Veronica's room was open. Her bed was empty, the lights out, so she must be in the guest house.

Unless Girl's Night had devolved to mani-pedis upstairs.

Unlikely, since Bailey wasn't much of a mani-pedi girl and she was heading up to Cole and Olivia's tomorrow to ride with Alex.

But Brit and Billie Rose together?

Bailey liked to joke about *my* corrupting influence, but those two women were menaces.

Still, when I went upstairs, our bedroom was empty, as was the bath, and the chair she liked to sit in while she was reading—its twin in the family room downstairs.

Her chairs, she'd declared with a smile when she sat in them the first time.

Like I gave a shit.

She could have every single chair in the house, if only she kept giving me that cat ate the canary smile, kept sucking me off as "payment."

My lips curving, I toed off my shoes, changed into sweats, and tugged on a hoodie.

They must be down in the guest house and I was going to crash their party.

I needed Bailey—in my arms, her body against mine, her lips tangling with mine, her body...I needed every single part of her.

My steps were quiet as I headed back downstairs, moving through the darkened hallway, out the back door, into the night air.

Spock greeted me, which was weird because he was usually glued to Bailey's side. But if she'd fallen asleep, she could have accidentally left him out. I scratched his head and together, we rounded the pool we'd had fenced so there was no risk of Alex getting hurt on his treks between main house and guest house.

Heading to Veronica's place, frowning when I saw that it was dark.

Maybe Bailey had passed out on the couch—it certainly wouldn't be the first time I'd retrieved her, carrying her back into the house, back into our bed.

A curl of heat through my middle, stroking down, wrapping around my cock like her fingers always instinctively did when we were in bed, when I woke her slowly with gentle kisses, slow and deep caresses.

Yeah, I wanted to do that.

But when I pushed into the guest house, using the code on the keypad that we'd set up, Bailey wasn't on the couch.

Now that curl of head had become a curl of worry.

Spock whined.

And, yeah, this was weird. He was usually right there inside with her, napping on her feet.

Quietly, I moved down the hall, maybe they were in Veronica's room? Not out of the question if she wasn't feeling well. Maybe—

The door was open and I peeked inside.

That curl became a tangled knot of worry.

Veronica's bed was empty. The bathroom the same. Alex's bedroom also unoccupied. They weren't in the back yard or the guest rooms in the main house.

"Come on, bud," I called, patting my leg, knowing Spock would follow as I continued looking.

But Veronica and Bailey weren't out front.

They...weren't *anywhere.*

"What the fuck?" I whispered, but then I remembered Billie Rose and Brit. Maybe the terrible twosome had convinced the women to go somewhere—out for a drink or desserts or—

I realized I was being stupid and tugged out my cell, dialed Bailey.

The call connected.

Rang.

And I heard her phone ringing down the hall.

Rushing to the front door, I saw that it was sitting on the little table there, my name on the screen.

That wasn't anything bad, I knew. She could have forgotten it.

But a sick feeling had settled in my stomach. The last time I'd felt this, she'd been trapped in a fucking wildfire and had nearly died.

My fingers rushing over the screen, I dialed Veronica.

Her phone rang from the kitchen.

"Fuck," I whispered.

I dialed another number and Billie Rose picked up, but worry filled her tone and replaced the confusion from my initial questions of asking where Bailey and Veronica were. "No," she said. "Brit was behind us, but she and Veronica were both planning to head off to bed when we left."

Pulse thundering in my veins, I called Brit.

There was still the option that they'd gone off together.

Except...

Brit hadn't seen them since she'd left Bailey waving at her on the driveway before she'd turned and returned to the house.

"Where are you?" I asked after I'd hung up, trying to think through the panic.

Alex was here, so I couldn't race off, couldn't jump in my car and start driving through the empty streets.

My phone rang and I jumped for it, hoping it was Bailey, that there was some explanation and she was going to be totally fine.

But it wasn't Bailey.

It was Brit.

"They're not at the Dairy," she said.

Fuck.

Where else? Where else could they be?

I inhaled, exhaled, tried to think this through, tried to reason it out.

But...where the fuck did I start?

"Did you check the Ring?"

"What?" I asked, the words not processing, not making any sense.

"Did you check your front door camera?"

No, I hadn't, but I put her on speaker, scrambled to open up the app, scrolling back through my search of the driveway, me and Alex pulling into the driveway. I saw her and Brit waving to Billie Rose and Dessie, realized I'd gone too far back.

Scrolled forward.

And then stopped, my heart pounding against my rib cage.

"Fuck."

"What?" Brit asked, her voice crackling through the speakers.

I watched the clip again, not quite able to acknowledge what I was seeing.

Then I processed what was on the video feed.

Processed what I was seeing.

And terror gripped me from head to toe.

"Call Pascal," I demanded. "Get him here."

And then I hung up on her and dialed 9-1-1.

FORTY-THREE

BAILEY

I really didn't like guns.

I really did not like them. I really did not the shiny silver death-bringers.

And great, now I sounded like a reject Dr. Seuss book.

But, bad sentence structure and missing rhymes aside, I had to use guns in the past and Gramps had made certain I was more than comfortable with them. But...I still didn't like them. Or maybe it was that I really didn't like that there was an object that could kill me in Candi's possession and I *really*, really didn't like it when it was pointed at Veronica.

Like now.

She waved the gun, drawing the barrel from me over toward Veronica, and shaking it vigorously in a way that sent a shiver down my spine.

If her finger slipped—

"Tie her up," Candi ordered V, now jerking the gun toward the chair that was rusty enough to look like it was going to give me tetanus...if I didn't get shot first.

When Veronica hesitated, the look that filled Candi's face scared me even more than the perpetual state of fear that I'd been existing in since I'd opened the front door to find this psycho standing on my porch. Quickly, not wanting to give Candi a chance for that finger to slip, I moved to the chair, sat down in it.

But though V followed me, she didn't immediately tie me up.

I looked over my shoulder at her, widened my eyes, silently telling her to listen to the psycho. Tie me the fuck up.

Like *now*.

Cooperation was important because I was trying to buy us some time, trying to come up with a plan. Veronica stalling and not following Candi's orders and getting herself—and in all likelihood me—shot was not the plan I was hoping to formulate.

My plan—which was, admittedly, still in process—had one key point.

Getting out of this alive.

Okay, two key points.

Because I was also hoping to get us away from Candi without getting shot.

Now, however, I wasn't sure that either of those were going to work out, especially if Veronica didn't get her ass out of the crosshairs.

"Do it," Candi ordered.

"I—"

"*Do it!*" Candi screeched.

Veronica's hands clenched on my shoulders, and I watched her teeth press into her bottom lip. "But..." she whispered. "With what?"

Ah.

Right.

It wasn't like there was a coil of rope, or a set of Billie's handcuffs at the ready.

The gun went off.

I screamed, and Veronica did too. Pain sliced through me, and for a second, I thought I'd been shot, that my plan was fucked and we were going to die then and there. But then I realized that it wasn't actually a bullet that had hit me. It was shards of concrete, the bullet having hit the wall all of a few feet in front of me.

V wavered behind me, her fingers clinging to my shoulders. "A-are you okay?"

"Yeah." I wiped a stinging spot on my temple, saw that my fingers came away with blood. Not an obscene amount, so that was something, but enough that I knew we were running out of time, plan or not. "You?"

"Fine."

"Think. *Think!*"

My eyes darted back to Candi and it was to see the other woman had begun pacing back and forth, the gun waving around, sometimes pointed at us, sometimes at the floor, sometimes perilously close to her own head as she stomped across the heavy concrete, yelling at herself.

"I need to do this," she said. "I need to do it and get out of here because they'll find me. Like they almost found me before."

They being Pascal, presumably.

Almost tracking Candi down, however, not being quite good enough, considering she was here with her gun and—

"Do it, Candi," she said, going full third person. "Do it. You need to take care of this because the fire didn't. She should have been ash by now. Ash and bone and—" She shook the gun violently. "She should have been *burned!*"

I glanced back to Veronica, my eyes wide.

Had she just said...

"So much burned, but not her! Why not *her?*"

"Shit," Veronica whispered.

And no, I hadn't heard wrong.

"The fire in River's Bend," I whispered back.

"Shit," V said again.

"Think!" Candi screamed, her hands coming to her head, fingers clawing into her hair.

Yeah, she'd totally lost it.

Only, maybe her losing it meant that we could use the time while she was stomping across the concrete floor, yelling into the ether to formulate a plan. Of course, I wasn't a fucking superhero and couldn't use sticky spiderwebs to shoot us toward the ceiling, couldn't teleport us out, couldn't fly through the air or shoot lightning bolts to knock Candi out. I just had me and V.

But neither of us were hurt.

No, we didn't have phones and I was presuming here, since I didn't know where we were, but I also thought it was safe to presume that Veronica also had no idea where we were. Candi had forced blindfolds on us on the drive over and had pulled her car into this warehouse.

Where there was nothing to see except concrete floors and walls.

A few bare lightbulbs turned on overhead.

A narrow strip of windows showing only darkness through the glass.

"Think!" Candi yelled again.

Yeah, seriously. *I* needed to think.

Because this was going to devolve sooner rather than later.

My vision had adjusted to the dark, and I scanned the large open room, spotting the rolling door she'd clearly opened and closed because her car was inside, a smaller steel door next to it. To the left of that I spotted a small office on the far side of the space. A rolling chair. A desk. Another of those small rectangular windows.

Was there a computer inside? Maybe a phone? A landline we could use to call for help?

I quietly pushed out of the seat.

"What are you doing?" V hissed, her hands sliding free of my shoulders.

"Shh." I waved her off, took a few silent steps to the side, trying to get a good look at that desk. If there *was* a phone, I could send V in to make a call, or maybe there was either exit through that room.

Candi was still yelling about burning me alive, acting totally unhinged...or more unhinged, anyway, so I took a chance and crept farther from the chair, peeking into the office.

And felt utter disappointment.

Because the desk was empty.

There was no extra exit.

It was just an almost empty room with a large L-shaped desk and a battered office chair, another of those narrow rectangular windows far above our heads.

Spinning back around, I nearly took out Veronica.

"What?"

V had the chair in her hand, the rusting halves having been folded against each other. Her eyes were a little wild, but she nudged me back into the office, closed the door, and then tucked the chair beneath the knob, angling it so the door couldn't be easily pushed in.

"V—"

She reached up, tugged off her scarf.

"Wh—"

Fingers in her pocket, brandishing something that had my heart skipping a bit, *my* eyes going wide.

She balled up the fabric, nodded determinedly.

"Shut up and listen to me. I have a plan."

FORTY-FOUR

AXEL

There were two police cars in the driveway, another two had taken off just a few minutes before, joining the others that were currently searching through the city.

Pascal had managed to get a license plate number from the video.

It was registered to one of Candi's aliases.

Now he was beating himself up, apologizing to me while dispatching his team, taking responsibility even though the only one they needed to blame was Candi.

She was the bitch who was obsessed with me for no good reason, the insane person who'd shown up and bundled Veronica and Bailey in her car like a fucking psychopath and now had taken them somewhere and—

"I fucked up," Pascal said quietly, his jaw tight enough that it looked ready to snap. "I put looking for her on the back burner with everything else that was going on. I didn't think she'd—"

He broke off and his eyes...fuck, they were filled with darkness. With agony.

"We all thought she'd finally had enough," I said. "None of us thought she would turn violent."

Showing up naked and trying to seduce me was leaps and bounds away from threatening my woman, from threatening Veronica with a weapon, from kidnapping both of them.

Apparently, it wasn't that evening.

"I fucked up," Pascal said again and his eyes...*fuck*.

The darkness that was in them, the horror and grief and *shadows* in his dark brown eyes threatened to take me to my knees.

I knew he'd been through something heavy, something dark.

I hadn't realized it was something like *this*.

I wanted his help. V and Bailey needed it.

But...I knew this was tearing him apart.

"I'll find them," he said and the quiet determination in his voice eased some of the worry. I had faith in him. I knew that he would come through.

At what cost to himself?

And yeah, I knew it was selfish, and maybe it added to my column of assholeness, but I wasn't going to let him to back out, wasn't going to save him that cost.

Because I'd do absolutely anything to save them.

Even if that meant putting a good man through something that was digging its fingers into the edges of a deep, painful wound, that was pulling on it and tearing it wide open and causing him even more pain.

I clamped a hand onto his shoulder. "I need you to focus."

His head jerked up, those agonized eyes locked with mine.

"I need you to help me find them." A beat. "Alive and whole. *I* need them. *Alex* needs them."

His throat worked.

His nostrils flared.

His hand came down on top of mine, clenching tightly.

Then he nodded. "I'll find them."

He broke my hold in a smooth move that told me I'd never be

able to hold my own with this man—at least not in a physical sense —even though I was bigger and heavier than him. He could kick my ass without a second thought.

A moment later, he was gone, melting into the shadows, and I knew that his disappearing skills would have made Bailey smile.

A thought that had agony blooming in my chest and slicing through my legs. I staggered backward, knees giving way, the thought of never getting to see her smile again sending me to my ass on the concrete. I dropped my head into my hands, trying to block out the fear, what might be a real possibility, trying to pretend there weren't cop cars in my driveway with flashing lights, Pascal and his team out searching.

Trying to pretend that Bailey and Veronica were just inside and asleep and—

The sound of an engine.

Jerking up, I expected to see another police car, or maybe to see one of Pascal's men pulling into the drive.

Instead, it was an older dark gray model that looked familiar, though I couldn't place it.

I didn't know where I'd seen the sedan that was stained with mud and dirt and—

The car slid to a halt and the doors flew open.

And...

My eyes didn't process wasn't what I was seeing.

Couldn't.

But my body felt the touch.

Felt *Bailey's* touch—her arms coming around me, her body slamming into mine.

She smelled like smoke and ash and there was blood on her face, a combination that immediately had terror gripping my insides and slicing deeply.

"I'm okay," she murmured. "I promise."

Her words didn't process, not at first.

Not until she pulled back and cupped my face and stared deep into my eyes.

"I'm okay, honey."

"You're bleeding," I rasped.

"Bailey!"

Pascal ran out of the shadows, skidding to a stop next to us. Bailey jerked back, tugging herself out of my arms.

I growled, started to reach for her, wanting to hold her, needing to make sure she was really okay.

Because—

That was when I realized that Veronica was still at the door.

She looked like she was okay. No blood, though her face was streaked with ash. But she wasn't wearing her scarf. I frowned. She hadn't lost all of her hair, and I thought she still looked beautiful, even with the closely cropped curls. But I knew she was insecure about it, and she wouldn't willingly take it off.

Stupid to be fixated on a scarf.

But my brain was moving slowly. It had been whipping around in a frenzy since the moment I'd seen the clip on the Ring camera. Now, it was barely able to process that Bailey had just driven up, that Veronica was there and okay too.

"You're okay," Pascal said, jerking my mind to the side again, yanking me to focus.

She *was* okay.

They were okay.

"Yeah," Bailey said softly, no doubt seeing that darkness in his eyes. She squeezed Pascal's hand. "We're both okay."

"What happened?" I asked, stepping close, wanting to tug her back into my arms but trying to control myself.

"Where's Candi?" he asked, and yeah, that was the more prudent of questions.

"Um..." Bailey said and fuck, why was there guilt on her face?

Why had happened that she would feel guilty about?

"What?" Pascal asked sharply.

And yeah, I thought that tone was prudent as well.

"Yeah, well"—she cleared her throat—"Candi was going a little crazy. She was waving the gun around and shot at us and so..." Her gaze drifted to the side. "We kind of burned down a warehouse."

"*What?*" Pascal and I snapped.

The officers who'd stayed behind had split up, two coming toward us, two approaching Veronica.

Who was moving.

To the trunk.

"Candi was being crazy, and we were able to lock ourselves into the office, but there was no way out. But V had that lighter"—she'd found that some medicinal marijuana helped with the pain—"and so we used her scarf thinking that we could sneak out in the smoke."

A wince.

"Turns out the walls in the office weren't concrete like the other ones and once the desk caught fire..."

Sweet Jesus.

Pascal rubbed his head.

The officers had reached us, and I saw their brows lift.

"We couldn't fit out the windows, but there was a lot of smoke, so we had to go out into the main area and—" She cleared her throat, voice dropping. "I freaked out a little bit when the smoke came in. Because"—teeth in her bottom lip—"well," she whispered. I took her hand, squeezing it tight. "You know. Veronica was...hell, she was *amazing.*"

Veronica had come over and she slid close to Bailey, wrapping her arm around Bailey's shoulders. "*You* were amazing. *I* was an idiot. The fire got out of control in seconds. We couldn't breathe or see and then Candi came out of nowhere—"

"You're the one who hit her with the chair."

"Wait, what?" one of the officers said.

"She had a gun," Veronica said quickly. "And tried to kidnap us." A shake of her head. "Well, she *did* kidnap us. But then she wanted to kill Bailey because she'd failed in the fire."

"The fire at the warehouse?" the officer asked, making notes on their pad.

"No," Bailey said, her fingers tightening. "The fire she started in River's Bend."

I inhaled.

So did the people around us.

"I always wondered why it started by my ranch." Her eyes came to mine, tears in sad brown depths. "She was trying to get rid of me so that—"

Thudding.

And yelling.

And more ridiculously loud *thudding*.

"What the fuck?" one of the officers asked.

The pair that had gone to Veronica first had moved to the car's trunk.

"Um," the other officer said.

Bailey bit her lip. "Veronica knocked her unconscious with the chair," she whispered. "But we couldn't leave her there, even though Veronica's plan was working way too well."

"*Your* plan?" I asked V archly.

"I didn't say it was a *good* plan." Veronica shrugged. "And in fairness," she muttered, showing a bloodthirstiness that I wouldn't have expected from her, a savage streak that I appreciated, "before you ask, I was all for leaving Candi behind. Bailey was the one who wanted to save her."

I glanced at the woman I loved, my fury surely written on my face. What the fuck had she been *thinking*?

"I couldn't leave her to burn up," she whispered. "I just couldn't. Not after—"

Not after all she'd been through.

Even though the woman had been happy to do the same to Bailey.

Hell.

I loved my crazy, kind, lovely woman.

"She was still unconscious," she whispered. "I didn't want to put her in the trunk, but we didn't have time to think of anything different, and we couldn't risk her free in the car..."

Veronica squeezed her shoulders. "The trunk was all we had."

The thudding got louder.

Was joined by intense screaming.

"Right," the shorter of the officers said. "We should probably deal with that"—a nod to the trunk—"and come back for your statements later."

The other office nodded.

And then they were moving off.

Joining their coworkers at the trunk.

Candi's screams grew louder when the police popped the trunk a few minutes later, guns out and at the ready. There was a scramble of movement, intense orders from the officers, and then Candi was in handcuffs and being shoved into the back of the police cruiser.

"Why do our stories always start with handcuffs?" Bailey whispered.

"Start?" I asked, running out of patience and tugging her into my arms, holding her tight again. "I thought this was the happy ending."

She cupped my jaw. "No," she whispered. "This is just the beginning of our story."

I inhaled sharply, eyes stinging. "Fuck, buttercup."

"I'm okay," she said again.

"I know," I whispered into her ear and then, because I still needed to reassure myself. "You survived." And then because she was okay, because she was here, I bent, kissed her hard and long, needing to know she was here and okay and still my Bailey, still the woman I loved, still the person that was the other half of my soul. I pulled back, chest heaving, hands going to her cheeks, forcing her to hold my gaze. "And I am never *ever* letting you go."

"Of course not." Her other hand holding my face, her eyes on mine. "I won't ever leave you," she vowed. "Not when I have one ounce of fight left in me."

"No," I said, finally, *finally* able to breathe. Finally able to smirk at her in the way I knew she loved. Able to tease because I knew she needed a moment of light. "Because we have that story to build."

"Exactly." A beat, her lush lips turning up. "And it involves lots and lots of handcuffs."

Epilogue

BAILEY, A YEAR LATER

I t had taken too fucking long.

But the houses were done.

I wasn't cut out for construction.

I especially wasn't cut out for the construction of two houses and a barn while simultaneously going to school and helping take care of a newly turned six-year-old with a boyfriend who was an assistant captain for a professional hockey team and—

"Bailey! Look at me!"

I grinned at Alex.

That new six-year-old.

He was still horse crazy, and yeah, I'd gone a little crazy for his last birthday, buying him a lovely mare with a gentle disposition.

Who he'd named Chewy.

Chewy!

Mixing up the *Wars* and the *Trek* and stabbing at my nerdy little heart.

I was never going to forgive Axel for showing him those movies.

He was a traitor, waltzing in and undoing my nerdy prep, getting him hooked on all things *Star Wars*.

Worse?

Veronica now had a horse named Han.

Han and Chewy.

Shoot me now.

I shivered, the memories of a year ago threatening to be called forth. Axel and Veronica and Alex and Brit and Billie Rose and Dessie and...a whole host of people had helped me put the trauma of my previous summer behind me. Well, they'd helped along with therapy, but both had enabled me to continue looking forward.

Along with Candi being in jail.

She'd admitted to starting the blaze in River's Bend to Veronica and me in the warehouse, but she'd also screamed it at the officers during their interrogation and hadn't tried to deny it when they'd managed to calm her down.

As a result, she was on trial for multiple counts of murder.

People had died in the fire.

She'd set it.

Add in charges for kidnapping...

And the case had been stacked against her.

Luckily for us, for the town, for the surviving members of Tom, Hank, and Eli's families, we hadn't been subjected to a trial.

She'd pleaded guilty in exchange for life in prison, in exchange for skipping out on a long, drawn-out trial.

I didn't have to worry about opening the door and finding her there.

Not now. Not ever.

Add in the gate and fences and extra security that Pascal had insisted on installing, I was safe.

My family was safe.

So, we'd been able to live.

Alex had started school *and* hockey (and no surprise, he was a natural at the latter and still a good student in the former).

Veronica had finished her treatment—three rounds of chemo, two of immune therapy.

Her last scan had been a month before and there was no sign of cancer.

The ranch had been in good hands, thanks to the manager that Axel had hired, and now I found that I could truly enjoy being up at Russet Ranch, riding Data, hearing the whoosh of the grass, feeling the sun, getting Picard and Data back up here, bringing Spock when we came on our regular visits.

This was now a place of happiness, rather than a heavy burden I would never dig my way out of.

Because of Axel and Veronica and Alex.

Because of Billie Rose and Dessie and Brit.

Because of school and a future job at River's Bend High.

Because of a town that looked after each other and a hockey family I could rely on and...

I belonged.

I'd found my place and my people and it was more than I could have ever dreamed about.

"It's great, isn't it?" Axel murmured, his arm snaking around my middle, tugging me against his side.

"I haven't forgiven you."

He smirked down at me, kissed the tip of my nose. "You love having a full barn, even if the new horses are messing up your naming convention."

"Just saying," I grumbled. "If you'd showed him the Chris Pine *Star Trek* movies he would have been hooked on those instead of all that *Wars* nonsense."

"You like that *Wars* nonsense."

I did.

Which was the worst of it. Because *I* was a traitor, too.

Not copping to that, though.

Nope. No freaking way.

Instead, I flounced over to our porch—with plenty of posts for handcuffs to be used—and scooped up the bag I'd brought.

The most important belonging that needed to be here.

Gramps's horseshoe.

Axel had saved it from the ashes...just like he'd saved me.

Smiling, I gently tugged it from the bag, turning to mock glare at the man who held my heart. "Put your lazy hockey butt to good use and help me hang this."

"My buttercup is so into butts."

Because he had a great one.

But I wasn't going to let him get away with that.

"No," I said, picking up the hammer and small box of nails I'd also brought with me, "that's you."

A nip to the top of my ear. "True," he murmured, smoothing his hand down my back, over my ass, squeezing the round globe.

I held up the horseshoe, positioned it just so. "Help me nail this."

A rough chuckle. "I thought I did that last night."

How did this man always make me melt?

Probably because that rough chuckle reminded me exactly *how* he made me melt, how good it felt, how—

Focus.

"Axel," I warned, glaring at him over my shoulder.

"Fine," he grumbled, bending and snatching up the hammer and nails.

"I ordered one for Alex and Veronica's place," I murmured as he positioned the first nail, tapping it in so that the horseshoe wouldn't fall. "It's not the same as this one." He went to work on the second nail. "But it's made by the same local artist," I said, voice softening. "I wanted them to be able to have something from Gramps and Gran too."

Axel kissed the back of my neck. "They're going to love it."

I knew they were.

Because we were family and Veronica and Alex had never made

me feel like an outsider, even though I wasn't connected to them by biology.

I was Alex's second mom.

Hands down.

No qualifications.

People who were kidnapped together...

Grinning, I know that it was more to do with the fact that I loved them both without reservations and they returned the affection. Our family was far from traditional.

But it was ours.

And I couldn't wait to add to it, to expand it, through biology or not—through friends big and small and kids who weren't of my womb (and maybe, someday, those that were) and plenty of annoying, pesky hockey players.

All would be welcome.

Because I'd found a place I belonged, and I wanted to make sure there was plenty of room for all those who didn't have that.

Realizing Axel hadn't finished with the last couple of nails, I spun to face him.

And froze.

Because Axel was kneeling behind me.

Ring box in hand.

I inhaled sharply.

"I love you to distraction, buttercup," he murmured, his eyes so fucking warm that I wanted to dive into them like warm ocean water. "Marry me?"

My lips parted, breath sliding out, head feeling a little fuzzy.

Another tie.

Another connection.

Another way to belong.

"Axel," I murmured, tears gathering on my lashes.

"I had a big speech planned," he said, the giant diamond glinting in the late afternoon sunlight. "With all sorts of fluffy words and heartfelt declarations. But"—he set the ring box down —"I know that you already know I'm in this for life."

I nodded.

Because I did know that.

"So," he went on, "I'll just go with what makes you smile, buttercup, because seeing you grin at me is the best part of my day. *Always*." He lifted his other hand, the one that had been behind his back.

When I saw what he held, I *did* smile.

And I also laughed.

He rose, clicking one half of the cuffs around my wrist, securing the other around his.

The metal ring was cool on my skin.

But my heart was beyond warm in my chest.

"I'm keeping you," I said, leaning close and pressing my lips to his. "For always."

He kissed me long and deep and slow.

Then I had another ring on.

This one on my finger.

"For always."

———

BILLIE ROSE

I set the basket quietly on Thelma's porch, not wanting the older woman to have the chance to reject the offering.

Thelma was stubborn.

She was also not eating enough.

How did I know this?

River's Bend had one grocery store and a handful of restaurants.

Her grocery purchases weren't coming frequently enough or in big enough quantities to sustain an adult woman.

Even one with a small appetite.

So, River's Bend would look after her.

But I knew that Thelma would accept the basket of food and toiletries if there was an opportunity to reject it, to take it and shove it back in my arms.

That was okay.

I could be sneaky.

It went perfectly with knowing all.

Lips curving, I hit the doorbell and then dashed down off the porch and along the grass, dodging the sensor for the automatic flood light (see? I really did know all) that was mounted near her garage. Triggered, it would illuminate the entire front yard and blow my cover.

But I was well-practiced in the art of ding dong ditch.

Moments later, I was safely behind a tree, watching Thelma look around, sigh, and eventually bring the basket inside.

Mission accomplished.

Mentally, I high-fived myself then walked down the quiet sidewalk, heading back to my car. I'd parked it around the corner to help with my sneakiness, but I didn't mind the trek. Not when the night sky was clear and the air was cool on my cheeks and I was taking care of my people.

My town was slowly putting itself back together.

But it would never be exactly what it had been before.

That was okay.

Change was good—ha. I could barely think that, let alone internalize it.

I liked to be in control. I liked things (and people) to stay in place in the carefully thought-out buckets I'd created. Change could derail that.

Especially when I wasn't the driving force of it.

Alas, I couldn't control all (something my friends and family would be shocked to know I thought).

It was something I knew, though.

I might be pushy and confident and demanding and know what I wanted, but I knew myself, too. I knew my limits, knew that I had to give on *some* things.

Just not very many of them.

Grinning, I turned the corner, enjoying that night air, my tennis shoes soundless on the sidewalk. I needed to stop by City Hall before heading home. My inbox was full. My spreadsheets needed to be reviewed. The summer festival needed to be planned.

The work of the mayor was never done.

But that thought made my grin grow even bigger.

Because I loved what I did and I loved River's Bend and—

I froze, my grin fading.

Irritation.

God, always, *always* he filled me with irritation.

Something that was even more *irritating* than the man himself. Because I was supposed to be untouchable.

Unable to be irritated.

But Joel Marshall *always* got under my skin.

And right now, he was leaning back against my little SUV, his arms crossed, his lips curved up into a smile that I wanted to wipe of his face.

Either with my fist or some pithy, snarky comment.

Preferably my fist.

Except, he was tall so his lips would be hard to reach. And he was big and solid and a hockey player who could probably crush me without breaking a sweat.

So, unfortunately, as it had been in the years that I'd known him, it would have to be with snark.

Irritatingly, the annoying hockey player beat me to the punch.

"Whatcha doing, harpy?"

Ugh.

If he knew how much that nickname made my blood boil, he would probably never use anything else.

As it was, he already used it enough to needle me, I was already thinking about punching him.

Or kissing—

No.

Stop *right* there.

I would not think of Joel and kissing. He was annoying and irritating and constantly needled me.

"Move," I said.

He kept his arms crossed, left his hip pinning the driver's side door closed. "I asked you a question."

See? Annoying.

Expecting that I owed him an answer.

"*Move*," I repeated.

He uncrossed his arms, but didn't shift, didn't move away from my door, and—this was something that would surprise people as well—I was tired.

I. Was. Tired.

That wasn't the Billie Rose everyone knew, certainly not the Billie Rose this annoying man knew.

But it was the truth.

And I might be a lot of things, but I always at least tried to be honest with myself.

In the year since the fire that had torn through my town, I'd been fighting to get us back on track and put back together. There were a lot of people who needed a lot of things, and I loved them and *wanted* to help them, so I'd been running full-tilt. Because I needed to get our town back to the old River's Bend, at least as much as would be possible.

It was just...

I wasn't entirely sure that was possible anymore.

I wasn't entirely sure that *I* could make that happen.

"Rosie?"

The soft, husky voice had me blinking, realizing that my eyes were stinging, that I was dangerously close to crying.

Stupid.

A hand on my arm, Joel's body shifting closer.

Good. He'd moved off the door and now I had an opening to escape (something else that would surprise people—that I frequently found myself in the position of needing to escape this man).

Not going there.

Inhaling silently, exhaling just as quietly, I bleeped the locks, shook off his hand, and reached for the handle.

"Rosie, baby—"

I yanked the door open, nearly taking his head off.

But freedom was near and my seat was within reach and—

That hand found my arm again and he tugged me back out of the opening, spinning me toward him. "What are you—?"

The question just halted, not giving me anything to rebuff.

And I found out the reason why approximately two seconds later.

Because his hand came to my cheek.

And his thumb brushed the underside of each eye.

I saw the glint of the tear perched on that rough finger and nearly died of embarrassment.

I was Billie Rose, mayor of River's Bend and badass extraordinaire. I didn't cry.

Except, he had the evidence right there on his thumb.

Panic welled up in my belly and I started to turn away—

Was stopped by that big, rough, *warm* hand.

His palm came to my face. "Rosie," he rasped, drawing my body to his.

Lips parting. Mouth coming close enough for me to feel the hot, dampness of his breath on my skin. Fingers flexing on my cheek.

And...

That was when I used my last avenue of escape.

My fingers found the panic button on my key fob.

And pressed.

———

Thank you for reading! I hope you loved meeting Axel and Bailey! The next book in the Rush Hockey series is book one of Billie Rose and Joel's story. LOVE, PUCKS, AND OTHER STORIES NOW>. **I hated hockey players. But I especially hated that I wanted one...**

CLICK HERE TO GET LOVE, PUCKS, AND OTHER STORIES NOW>

And if you enjoyed SO PUCKING OVER IT, you'll love the sexy, sweet, and close-knit Breakers Hockey crew. The first book in the series, BROKEN, is now live!

It is sexy, hot, adorable and such a fun read. You will not be able to put this down!" —Amazon Reviewer

———

I so appreciate your help in spreading the word about my books, including sharing with friends! Please leave a review on your favorite book site!

You can also join my Facebook group, the Fabinators, for exclusive giveaways and sneak peeks of future books.

SIGN UP FOR ELISE FABER'S NEWSLETTER HERE: https://www.elisefaber.com/newsletter

Rush Hockey

Big Puck Energy
Filthy Puckboy
So Pucking Over It
Love, Pucks, and Other Stories

———

Hate missing Elise's new releases? Love contests, exclusive excerpts and giveaways?

Then signup for Elise's newsletter here!

http://eepurl.com/bdnmEj

———

And join Elise's fan group, the Fabinators (https://www.facebook.com/groups/fabinators) for insider information, sneak peaks at new releases, and fun freebies! Hope to see you there!

———

Breakout

Checked

Coasting

Centered

Charging

Caged

Crashed

A Gold Christmas

Cycled

Caught

Cap

Covered

Breakers Hockey (all stand alone)

<u>Broken</u>

<u>Boldly</u>

<u>Breathless</u>

<u>Ballsy</u>

Rush Hockey

Big Puck Energy

Filthy Puckboy

So Pucking Over It

Love, Action, Camera (all stand alone)

Dotted Line

Action Shot

Close-Up

End Scene

Meet Cute

Love After Midnight (all stand alone)

Rum And Notes

Virgin Daiquiri

On The Rocks

Sex On The Seats

Life Sucks Series (all stand alone)

Train Wreck

Hot Mess

Dumpster Fire

Clusterf*@k

FUBAR

Roosevelt Ranch Series (all stand alone, series complete)

Disaster at Roosevelt Ranch

Heartbreak at Roosevelt Ranch

Collision at Roosevelt Ranch

Regret at Roosevelt Ranch

Desire at Roosevelt Ranch

Phoenix Series (read in order)

Phoenix Rising

Dark Phoenix

Phoenix Freed

Phoenix: LexTal Chronicles (rereleasing soon, stand alone, Phoenix

world)

From Ashes

In Flames

To Smoke

KTS Series (all stand alone, series complete)

Riding The Edge

Crossing The Line

Leveling The Field

Scorching The Earth

Cocky Heroes World

Tattooed Troublemaker

About the Author

USA Today bestselling author, Elise Faber, loves chocolate, Star Wars, Harry Potter, and hockey (the order depending on the day and how well her team -- the Sharks! -- are playing). She and her husband also play as much hockey as they can squeeze into their schedules, so much so that their typical date night is spent on the ice. Elise is the mom to two exuberant boys and lives in Northern California. Connect with her in her Facebook group, the Fabinators or find more information about her books at www.elise-faber.com.

f facebook.com/elisefaberauthor

a amazon.com/author/elisefaber

BB bookbub.com/profile/elise-faber

O instagram.com/elisefaber

d tiktok.com/@elisefaberauthor

g goodreads.com/elisefaber